BBC
DOCTOR WHO

Deep Time

BBC

DOCTOR WHO

Deep Time

Trevor Baxendale

B\D\W\Y
BROADWAY BOOKS
NEW YORK

Copyright © 2015 by Trevor Baxendale

All rights reserved.
Published in the United States by Broadway Books,
an imprint of the Crown Publishing Group,
a division of Penguin Random House LLC, New York.
www.crownpublishing.com

BROADWAY BOOKS and its logo, B\D\W\Y, are trademarks of
Penguin Random House LLC.

This edition published by arrangement with BBC Books, an imprint of
Ebury Publishing, a division of the Random House Group Ltd.

Doctor Who is a BBC Wales production for BBC One. Executive producers:
Steven Moffat and Brian Minchin.

BBC, DOCTOR WHO, AND TARDIS (word marks, logos and devices)
are trademarks of the British Broadcasting Corporation and are used
under license.

Library of Congress Cataloging-in-Publication Data is available upon request

ISBN 978-1-101-90579-1
eBook ISBN 978-1-101-90580-7

Printed in the United States of America

Editorial director: Albert DePetrillo
Series consultant: Justin Richards
Project editor: Steve Tribe
Cover design: Lee Binding © Woodlands Books Ltd 2015
Production: Alex Goddard

2 4 6 8 10 9 7 5 3 1

First U.S. Edition

For Martine, Luke and Konnie
— with love and thanks for all the time

Prologue

The ship gleamed in the starlight, a gold and amber dream of a ship, with tailfins splayed like the wings of a dove preparing for flight. It was waiting patiently, sitting on three short, inclined landing supports, boarding ramp down, ion thrusters glowing.

Raymond Balfour crossed the wide concourse leading to the space dock and decided it was the most beautiful ship he'd ever seen. He had owned many before this one – some had been gifts, others he had bought, and they were all special – but this one was unique.

For one thing, it had been made to order. It was expensive; all spacecraft were expensive, but more so when they were custom built in the private shipyards of Far Station. Secondly, it had been built for a particular purpose; this was no pleasure cruiser, although anyone could be forgiven if at first glance they believed it was a rich man's luxury yacht or spar. Thirdly, the purpose was a mission; a journey of exploration that promised the discovery and crossing of new frontiers.

Balfour paused when he reached the edge of the space

dock platform. The ship rose above him, glittering and eager for flight. Etched in silver letters across the golden bows was the name: *Alexandria*. Balfour had chosen the name himself; it meant smart, daring and fearful of nothing.

It was perfect.

Beyond the *Alexandria* was a brilliant star field streaked with the scarlet blaze of an ancient supernova. And beyond that, the edge of the galaxy. Beyond that… the unknown.

Balfour trembled with excitement.

'Excuse me, sir,' said a large, angular service robot politely. It towered over Balfour, even when bowing respectfully.

'What is it, Trugg?'

'The research team are all assembled, sir. The ship is ready for departure.'

Balfour nodded. 'I know, Trugg. I know. I just want to savour the moment.'

Trugg straightened patiently. 'Very good, sir.'

Balfour stood and drank in the sight before him, allowing his eyes to roam the long, amber lines and smooth golden hull. 'Tell me, Trugg. When you look at the *Alexandria* – what do you see?'

'A spacecraft, sir.'

'Do you know what I see?'

'A spacecraft, sir?'

'I see adventure!'

'Very good sir,' Trugg replied. 'May I suggest that we join the boarding party? Professor Vent is very keen to leave.'

*

'You're late,' said Professor Tabitha Vent. 'We were due to leave an hour ago.'

Raymond Balfour strolled up the *Alexandria*'s boarding ramp wearing his billionaire's smile. 'Relax, Professor! Or may I call you Tabitha?'

'Nearly everyone calls me Tibby, as a matter of fact,' she replied. 'Seems like less of a mouthful.' She was as tall as Balfour, and around the same age, perhaps a little older. It was hard to tell, because Balfour was rich enough to afford all the latest rejuvenation techniques. Tibby guessed he probably had shares in Spectrox, but then she wasn't feeling in a very generous mood. She was suddenly conscious of wearing week-old space fatigues with her hair tied up in a rough ponytail. She had come straight from a dig on Ursa Minor. Balfour looked like he'd come straight from the salon.

Balfour waved cheerfully at the small group of researchers and scientists standing behind Tibby. 'Hello there. Everyone ready?'

Everyone said they were.

'You were supposed to be here an hour ago,' said Tibby. Although she was nominally at the head of the research team, she hardly knew some of the people standing behind her. Nevertheless she felt compelled to speak for them all. 'My team have been kept waiting. The crew have been kept waiting. *I've* been kept waiting!'

Balfour smiled the smile of a man for whom timekeeping and schedules had never meant much, if anything.

His large servitor robot clambered up the spaceship boarding ramp and stooped to pass through the airlock.

The robot was carrying a lot of expensive luggage.

'Take that straight through to my cabin, Trugg,' said Balfour.

'Very good, sir,' answered the robot, lumbering slowly forward. 'Excuse me, madam.'

Tibby was forced to move out of the robot's way. 'Is there really any need for all that luggage?' she sighed. 'We're supposed to be travelling light. This is a scientific expedition, not a holiday.'

'I'm well aware of that, Professor. I am paying for the expedition, after all.'

Balfour was smiling, but Tibby got the point. 'Yes, well, of course we all owe a great deal to you, Mr Balfour. It's just that we've been waiting such a long time to mount an expedition like this and we're impatient to begin.'

'There's really no need to worry,' Balfour said. 'I spoke to the spaceport master. He agreed to give us a little longer in dock before we have to leave.'

'My research team are all here. You are here. The crew is on board and the ship is ready to leave. Must we delay any longer?'

Balfour glanced back down the *Alexandria*'s boarding ramp as if he was expecting someone else to walk in at any moment. 'Just a minute or two more, if you please. I'm waiting for the last members of our team to arrive.'

'The team is here!' Tibby said, exasperated. 'There *is* no one else!'

At that moment two people came hurrying up the boarding ramp and burst onto the deck.

'Sorry we're late!' said a very pretty young woman as

she came to a halt. She was a little out of breath, as if she had been running.

'Who the devil are you?'

'I'm Clara,' the woman said. 'And this is the Doctor.'

A very tall, rather gaunt man with an unruly shock of grey hair stepped forward. 'Right,' he said, his piercingly cold eyes sweeping around the cabin. 'Now I'm here we can begin. I do hope you're all ready to be terrified!'

Chapter

1

Half an hour earlier Clara Oswald had been finished for the day. She had a banging headache after a double lesson with the most recalcitrant Year 10 group she had ever taught but she still welcomed the extra-loud jangle of the final school bell.

The prospect of an evening spent marking GCSE comprehension exercises was a relief in itself. At least her flat was quiet. No interruptions, no banter, no yelling, no school bell... Just a mug of tea, a pile of books, and then maybe a glass of Prosecco at the end of it.

But then a familiar wheezing and groaning noise heralded the arrival of an old blue police box out of thin air and she knew any plans she had could, as her gran might say, 'Go to pot!'

The Doctor stuck his head out of the TARDIS. 'Psst! Fancy a quick trip to another galaxy?'

It was the kind of invitation that Clara never wanted to turn down. Not any more. The Doctor's time machine could have her back at her flat before she'd even left Coal Hill School and there would be time enough for marking.

Now Clara was in the far future, standing on the deck of a spaceship as it blasted off from a docking station a hundred thousand light years from Earth. Sometimes it was hard to get your bearings.

'Where are we again?' she asked. 'Exactly?'

'The deep-space private research vessel *Alexandria*. All mod cons. We're on a mission to find a lost wormhole in space.'

'We are?'

The Doctor glanced crossly at her. 'I thought I told you all this in the TARDIS. Weren't you listening?'

Clara opened her mouth to reply but it was too late. The Doctor was already talking again. 'Small crew, team of research scientists, I've managed to wangle an invite. Let me do all the talking.'

'As if I had a choice.'

'Just smile and try to look intelligent.'

Clara pursed her lips. 'Try?'

'Just do your best.'

The giant servitor robot that had carried Raymond Balfour's luggage on board clanked back through the doorway leading to the rest of the ship. It had to stoop again, servomotors whirring quietly and efficiently.

'Excuse me, sir,' the robot said, addressing Balfour. 'But there appears to be something untoward in the main cargo hold.'

Balfour frowned. 'What kind of something?'

'A police box, sir,' Trugg said. 'At least, that's what it says on the sign.'

'That'll be mine,' said the Doctor, stepping forward.

'Very important scientific equipment, vital to my work. Just leave it alone and it'll be fine.'

'How did you get it on board?' asked Balfour.

'Never mind about police boxes,' interrupted Tibby Vent. She pointed to the Doctor. 'Who is this man, exactly?'

'This is the Doctor,' explained Balfour. 'He's an expert on space-time travel.'

'Among other things,' added the Doctor.

'I've just signed him on to your team,' Balfour added.

'I don't need anyone else on my team,' Tibby said. 'Certainly not an "expert" in space-time travel!'

'Are you sure?' asked the Doctor. Tibby Vent stiffened visibly, clearly unused to being challenged. 'Come on now, Professor. You may have stumbled on the location of the oldest wormhole in existence but do you actually know how it works?'

'Don't be ridiculous.'

'I thought not.'

'I meant don't be ridiculous, I know full well how a wormhole works. It is a perfectly natural phenomenon.'

'There is nothing natural about this particular phenomenon,' the Doctor said.

By now everyone on deck was listening intently. Tibby Vent was completely irritated. 'What on earth are you talking about?'

'Nothing on Earth, I can assure you. There is nothing at all on that tiny little world that can possibly prepare you for what you will soon encounter.' The Doctor's cold gaze bored into her. 'That wormhole leads to the unknown, Professor. The absolute *unknown*.'

'I am a scientist, Doctor. It is my job to explore the unknown!'

'And it's my job to protect you from it.'

Raymond Balfour stepped forward with a smile. 'Perhaps it would be better if we continued this discussion later? Professor, Trugg can help you and your team find their cabins. I'll introduce the Doctor and Miss Oswald to the captain.'

It was a skilful bit of diplomacy, Clara thought, but it didn't stop Tabitha Vent eyeing the Doctor with obvious suspicion as Balfour led them away. Clara saw the robot, Trugg, introducing himself to the professor and then they disappeared from sight as they turned a corner.

'Professor Vent has rather a forthright personality,' Balfour explained. 'She's the best at what she does, but sometimes lacks the human touch.'

'I know the problem,' said Clara. 'Believe me.'

'She's heading up the research team, but we'll do the full introductions later,' Balfour said. 'I think you'll want to see around the *Alexandria* first. It's been designed and built to order, specifically for this mission.'

'Based on a *Heracles*-class Starcruiser, if I'm not mistaken,' said the Doctor.

'That's right, although we've added a few improvements. The ion thrusters have a forty-astron hyperdrive capacity. The hold is divided into state-of-the-art labs and research facilities with entoptic hologram displays. The living quarters and cabins are fully appointed with artificial gravity tuned to absolute Earth-normal throughout. Hull shielding has been upgraded to withstand five times the normal cosmic ray bombardment and heavy radiation…'

'It's beautiful,' Clara said.

'It must have cost a packet,' said the Doctor.

Balfour shrugged. 'The *Alexandria* is the most expensive deep-space private research vessel ever built – but I think she's worth it. We're ready for just about anything.'

'We'll see,' said the Doctor.

The *Alexandria* entered its natural habitat, the cold vacuum of space, like an eagle riding the warmest of thermals. Glittering under the arc lights of the docking port, the ship eased away from Far Station, away from the vast galaxy of stars behind it, and headed for deep space.

Clara could feel the faint hum of the engines through the soles of her shoes as they walked through the interior of the ship. Only thirty minutes earlier, she'd been standing on the old wooden floorboards of a classroom in Shoreditch, waiting to go home. Now she was hurtling through outer space, destined for… what?

She nudged the Doctor as they walked. 'Wormholes?'

'Conduits through time and space, linking one part of the universe to another.'

'Like a tunnel?'

The Doctor winced. 'No! Well, if you want to call a complex space-time event compressing billions of light years into a near singularity "a tunnel", then yes. I suppose so.'

'And what's so special about this wormhole, then?'

'It's very, very old. And like any tunnel that is very, very old, it's not necessarily safe to use.'

'And this lot are about to try and use it, are they?'

'I'm very much afraid so, Clara.'

'Then it's up to us to stop them, right? That's what we're here for?'

'No,' said the Doctor. 'We're here to help them.'

'This is the flight deck,' Balfour said as he led the Doctor and Clara through a wide bulkhead door. 'Captain Laker should have something rather special to show you.'

The flight deck was just like the rest of the *Alexandria* – sleek and humming with perfectly suppressed power. Ergonomic control consoles lined the sides and front of the deck, which was dominated by a panoramic hologram showing the way ahead.

In front of this, at the centre of the flight deck, was the captain's chair. The man sitting in it stood up as they came in and flashed what Clara considered a very nice smile. He wore what looked like a genuine leather jacket, which, with his good looks and short-back-and-sides, lent him a charmingly old-fashioned and rather heroic look.

Balfour introduced them and then departed, saying that he had to prepare for the mission briefing due to take place in the 'common room', which sounded a bit too much like a school staff room for Clara. She shook the memory of Coal Hill out of her head and concentrated on the here and now.

Captain Laker jerked a thumb at the hologram. 'You're just in time,' he said. 'We're about to leave the Milky Way.'

The hologram showed a shimmering field of purple-blue space, dotted with stars. It floated in the air like a bubble of space and looked so real that Clara wanted to reach out and touch it. 'It's so beautiful,' she said.

'The colours you can see are the remains of a star – a cloud of superheated gas, radiating outwards from a stellar explosion that took place millions of years ago. We're flying straight through it.'

The cloud changed from blue to lilac and then a deep mauve as the *Alexandria* sped onwards. Gradually it shifted to a startling red, then a darker crimson, bathing the occupants of the flight deck in the colour of blood.

'The very edge of the galaxy,' said the Doctor said quietly. 'This is all that's left of the last star before the void.'

The scarlet light suddenly faded and was replaced by a deep, impenetrable blackness. There was not a single star to be seen.

'We've left the galaxy,' Laker confirmed. 'It's quite a sight, isn't it?'

'I can't see anything,' said Clara, shivering a little. 'Just… darkness.'

'No more stars,' explained the Doctor. 'Not until the next galaxy, which is Andromeda. If Captain Laker increases the scanner magnification, we could see it from here, and many other galaxies too.'

Laker nodded. 'Yeah, I could, but where would the romance be in that?'

'Romance?' repeated Clara.

Laker gestured to the holoviewer again. 'Endless night. Nothing more romantic than that.'

'Or terrifying,' said the Doctor. 'How long until we reach the wormhole?'

'Well, we should reach maximum speed very soon. The approximate location is about fifty light years outside the galactic rim, so at a rough guess we could be there in another couple of hours.'

'How do you plan to find it?' the Doctor asked. 'You said the location is approximate.'

'That's where Jem comes in,' said Laker. He gestured towards the front of the flight deck.

Positioned almost beneath the hologram viewer was a long, low seat – almost a couch – surrounded by a cluster of instruments. Lights flickered across control panels and a profusion of wires led from the top of the couch to a transparent dome. Sitting under this, like a woman in an old-fashioned hair salon, was the most delicate-looking person Clara had ever seen. She had milky-smooth skin and elfin features and was dressed in a close-fitting overall with a high collar. Her large, almond-shaped eyes were wide open and completely white. Despite this, Clara got the distinct impression that they saw more than most human eyes.

'Our astrogator,' said Laker. He spoke softly, as if he didn't want to disturb her concentration.

'An augmented clone?' The Doctor didn't look too happy.

'Hello,' said the occupant of the couch. Her voice was quiet but musical. 'You must be the Doctor. And you are... Clara. I'm Jem 428. Pleased to meet you.'

'Hi,' said Clara, a little surprised. She didn't recall being introduced.

'I read your minds,' Jem explained with a smile. 'Don't worry – I'm only a very low-level telepath. Surface details only – no big secrets.'

'Well… that's good.'

'Jem's a clone, genetically engineered to be ultra-sensitive to the space-time continuum,' said the Doctor. 'They can hear what the universe has to say. At least, that's what they claim.'

'And she's also right here,' said Clara pointedly.

The Doctor frowned and then realised what she meant. He knelt down suddenly so that he was level with Jem 428's head. 'I'm so sorry. Hello, Jem. Tell me: what can you hear?'

Jem's perfectly white eyes stared straight ahead into the darkness of the holoviewer. 'I can hear the song of the stars and the distant whispers of the furthest galaxies…'

The Doctor glanced back up at Clara. 'She means she can sense the minute fluctuations in the gravitational field that exists between dark matter.'

'OK,' said Clara, taking a deep breath. 'While we're at it: dark matter?'

'It's invisible and makes up most of the universe, along with dark energy,' explained the Doctor. 'It's really only detectable by its gravitational effect on other matter. An astrogation clone can seek out the axion strings and nodes that exist only in dark matter and make it into a sort of mental map.'

'I think I prefer "the song of the stars",' said Clara.

'Suit yourself.'

'I can hear the call of the Phaeron Roads,' Jem breathed,

still staring into the void. Clara noticed that her eyes never seemed to blink.

The Doctor frowned deeply. 'Can you, indeed?'

'Fairy what?' asked Clara.

'Phaeron Roads,' repeated the Doctor, standing up. He looked at the view screen, his eyes boring into the depthless night. 'It's an old term. The name for a vast network of ancient wormholes that stretch across the entire universe.'

'You mean like the one we're heading for?'

'Exactly.' He looked thoughtful, his eyebrows knitting together. His long, craggy face was drawn, and Clara thought it would be easy to mistake his expression for anxiety if it weren't for the gleam of intense curiosity in his eyes.

'It might be best if Jem was left alone for a while,' said Laker. Clara had almost forgotten he was there. 'She finds it easier to work in the peace and quiet.'

The Doctor flashed the pilot a look that Clara couldn't quite understand. Was it discomfort? Disappointment?

'I think Mr Balfour wants everyone in the common room,' Laker said evenly. He held his hand out towards the exit. 'One deck down. You can't miss it.'

The Doctor looked again at Jem 428, lying prone in her couch beneath the transparent dome. 'All right,' he said, turning to leave with Clara. 'But we'll have words later, Captain.'

As the Doctor stalked off the flight deck, Clara glanced back at Laker. For someone in charge of the best and most expensive spaceship ever built, he looked distinctly troubled.

Chapter

2

The *Alexandria*'s common room was a circular chamber located near the centre of the ship. Clara thought it looked more like a posh hotel lounge than the common room of a scientific expedition.

Raymond Balfour was standing at the front with his robot, Trugg, waiting placidly nearby.

Professor Vent sat on a low settee, sipping a hot drink from a mug. Opposite her sat a young man with thin, swept-back hair and a rather supercilious expression. He put both feet up on a low coffee table and winked at the professor.

There were two other people sitting in the room; a younger woman with glossy black hair and matching jumpsuit, and a pale-looking, rather nervous man with a computer tablet clutched to his chest.

'Right,' announced Balfour. 'Now we're all here, it's time I introduced everyone properly.'

Clara sat down in an armchair next to the nervous-looking man with the tablet, but the Doctor stayed on his feet at the back of the room, where he could see everyone, leaning against the wall with his arms folded. Professor Vent muttered about what a waste of time all this was when she had important work to do. The man with his feet up smirked at her.

'You all know me...' Balfour began.

Clara hadn't met him until a half an hour ago but she knew his type; young-looking, if not actually young, smartly dressed and extremely wealthy. He wasn't bad-looking, in fact he was almost too good-looking, and she suspected plastic surgery or some futuristic equivalent. His teeth were perfect, his eyes were bright blue and he had a thatch of artfully tousled blond hair.

'My full name is Raymond Rueun Balfour the Third. But you can call me Ray. Welcome to the *Alexandria*. Hopefully you've had time to dump your stuff and get used to the layout. It's pretty straightforward. If you can't find anything, just ask. I'd like to think we're all friends here, or at least we soon will be. We're going to be spending a lot of time together over the next few weeks, after all.' He smiled happily, but his only reply was silence.

Not quite enough ice broken yet, Clara thought.

'I've got mission datapads for you all,' Balfour continued, and Trugg dutifully handed out a small tablet computer to each of them. 'It contains the full *Alexandria* specs, the mission parameters and, perhaps most importantly, a research team and ship's crew list and relevant biogs.'

Clara touched the screen of her tablet and a holographic display lit up. Icons floated in the air. She touched one, which turned out to be a list of the people on board:

```
FUNDING:
RAYMOND BALFOUR


RESEARCH TEAM:
TABITHA VENT    — research team leader
MARCO SPRITT    — archaeology
TANYA FLEXX     — medic / exobiology
LUIS CRANMER    — astrophysics

CREW:
DAN LAKER       — pilot
JEM 428         — astrogator
MITCH KELLER    — chief engineer
HARLEY HOBSON   - engineer
```

'I'm the least important person on that list,' Balfour continued. 'This whole thing, this entire expedition, is actually down to one person: Professor Tabitha Vent.'

Tabitha Vent gave an embarrassed wave as she was given a small round of applause. 'Call me Tibby,' she said. 'Tabitha is only for when I'm being told off.'

'Ladies and gentlemen,' Balfour said, 'allow me to formally introduce the Emeritus Professor of Extraterrestrial Studies at the University of New Earth. The professor is a renowned expert – the leading authority, in fact – on the ancient Phaeron race, as I'm sure you're all aware. Tibby was the lead translator on the Ganymede Stone project and she is responsible for finding and mapping the Phaeron Roads.'

The Doctor was listening intently, lips pursed in thought, his sharp eyes taking in every detail. Clara noticed the tiniest deepening of his frown at the mention of the Phaeron Roads.

'Perhaps Tibby could give us a little background on that,' Balfour said, 'and introduce the rest of her team.'

'I'm not much good at talking, to be honest,' Tibby said, standing up. 'I'm better with a pile of alien books and a translator program.'

She faced the room and the supercilious-looking man with his feet on the table eyed her carefully. It was quite clear that he appreciated what he saw.

'OK, very quick history lesson,' Tibby began. 'Millions of years ago there was a race called the Phaeron. They're completely extinct from the universe now, but we know they existed because of what they left behind: ancient ruins on a variety of planets throughout the galaxy, plus various bits and pieces of fossilised technomics. All evidence of what appears to have been a very advanced civilisation. Certainly they had space travel, that much is obvious, but the Phaeron were pretty much unique in that they got around the universe entirely by the use of wormholes. What's particularly interesting is that the Phaeron drew up a map of all these wormholes, a vast interconnecting network of space-time conduits spread throughout the cosmos. No one has ever known how to find them before because the Phaeron were very careful about keeping them secret.'

'How did *you* find them?' asked the Doctor.

'As Mr Balfour said, I worked on the Ganymede Stone. That's a Phaeron monument, or what's left of it, we found on the Jupiter moon ten years ago.'

The Doctor nodded, as if Tibby was simply confirming

something that he already knew. 'I've been there.' He hunched up his shoulders and gave a shiver. 'Chilly.'

'Very. We found the monument under about a kilometre of polar ice. There was an inscription in the stonework: Phaeron runes from the height of their powers, perfectly preserved. It was a translator's dream. I worked on it for six years once we'd dug the thing out. We found a ton of stuff: Phaeron biological data, technological plans, you name it, they left it.'

'And a map of the wormholes.'

'And a map, yes.'

'Convenient,' said the Doctor.

'Not really. Most of the wormholes were dead. Some kind of natural singularity collapse that caused a chain reaction across the galaxy, closing the conduits down one by one over the course of a million years or so. Put simply, they don't exist any more.'

'Except for this one,' said the Doctor. 'The one we're heading towards right now.'

'That's right,' said the young man with the sardonic expression. He swung his feet off the table and turned around in his seat to face the Doctor and Clara. 'And that's where I come in.'

'And you are?'

'Marco Spritt. You've probably heard of me already.'

'No. Should I have?'

Marco frowned. 'The search for the *Carthage*?' he prompted.

Clara looked from Marco Spritt to the Doctor. 'What's the *Carthage*?' she asked.

Marco looked aghast. 'You mean you've never heard of the *Carthage*?'

'We've been away from Earth for some time,' Clara said.

'At least half an hour,' the Doctor muttered.

'Well, as I was saying just before,' Marco said, 'this is where I come into the picture. The *Carthage* was the deep-space exploration vessel that *famously* disappeared over a century ago. It was charting the fringes of the galaxy when it simply vanished from space. It had a crew of seventy-seven, and every one of them was lost.'

'And you think it went into this wormhole thing?' Clara asked.

'Its last known location, based on the ship's transceiver signal, puts it right where Tibby's map shows the wormhole to be located. So yes, that's exactly what I think happened.' Marco sat forward, suddenly intent. 'The history of the *Carthage* – what might have happened to it, where it went, is really important to me.'

'Why is that?'

'The captain of the *Carthage* was Caitlin Spritt – my mother.'

'Ah,' said the Doctor, 'and it's not impossible that if your mum accidently flew the *Carthage* into the Phaerons' old wormhole, it could have ended up in the Andromeda galaxy. The crew of seventy-seven might be alive and well.'

Marco nodded. 'Yes.'

'So the combination of the professor's wormhole map and your interest in the *Carthage*'s disappearance have led you to... Raymond Rueun Balfour the Third?' The Doctor frowned. 'Not sure I see the connection.'

'We couldn't fund a mission like this ourselves,' Tibby admitted. 'The Phaeron are considered something of a backwater in galactic prehistory. The *Carthage*, while famous, is something of a pet project for Marco.'

Marco bristled at the words 'pet project'. 'It's a bit more than that, actually.'

'But you do have a very personal interest in it.'

'I heard about Tibby's research into the Phaeron and Marco's interest in the *Carthage* quite separately,' Balfour explained. 'So it was me who brought them together – and me who decided to fund a mission that might help both of them.'

'If Tibby and Marco are the drivers behind this little trip,' said the woman in the shiny black jumpsuit, 'then Luis and I are the hired help. Hi. I'm Dr Tanya Flexx – that's double X by the way – and the life and soul of the party here is Luis Cranmer.'

Cranmer nodded uncertainly and licked his lips without saying anything. He noticed Clara smile and immediately looked down at his datapad, scrolling through the hologram without seeing anything.

'If anyone's space sick, then I'm your best bet,' said Tanya. She looked at Cranmer and added, 'You'd better stick close to me, Luis.'

Cranmer gave her a weak smile but said nothing.

'And what about you two?' Tanya said, looking at the Doctor and Clara. She tapped her datapad with a well-manicured fingernail. 'You're not listed on here.'

'I thought they were the inflight entertainment,' Marco smirked.

'*Entertainment?*' repeated the Doctor, horrified.

'Well, you know… the clothes and whatnot. You look like a magician or something.'

The Doctor glanced down at his black frock coat and narrow trousers. 'I keep telling everyone – it's minimalist!'

'All right, keep your lovely curly hair on, sweetheart.' Tanya smiled mischievously. 'So who are you?'

'I'm the Doctor – but not your kind of doctor.'

'Are you a specialist?'

'Like you wouldn't believe. And this is Clara Oswald, my assistant—'

'Not his assistant,' said Clara.

'Not my assistant,' the Doctor corrected himself. 'My…'

'Friend?' Clara suggested.

'Associate.'

Clara raised an eyebrow at him for this, and the Doctor gave her a *well-what-else-could-I-say* shrug.

'Now that we're all introduced and properly under way,' announced Balfour, 'I propose a toast. Trugg?'

'Sir.' With great delicacy, the huge robot held out a tray of champagne flutes towards Clara.

Startled, but nevertheless delighted, Clara took one of the glasses. 'Thank you.'

Trugg moved around the lounge, proffering the tray to each in turn until everyone had a glass of champagne.

Balfour raised his glass. 'To the Phaeron Roads, and the last voyage of the *Carthage*.'

They all clinked their glasses together and drank. Clara noticed that Tanya Flexx downed hers in one gulp and gestured to Trugg for a refill. Luis Cranmer barely touched his. In fact he looked distinctly unwell.

Trugg recharged Tanya's glass and she took another sip of champagne. 'So what *is* your interest in all this, Doctor?'

The Doctor began to stalk slowly around the circumference of the room. 'What's my interest in all this? Well, I'm fascinated by the history of the Phaeron, of course, and certainly intrigued by the fate of the *Carthage*. But to be perfectly honest with you... neither matters one tiny jot.'

There was a sudden, difficult silence. The Doctor paused, his startlingly clear eyes looking at each of them in turn. 'I'm an expert in space-time travel. In fact I'm an expert in everything from Venusian aikido to yo-yos. I don't know if any of that stuff will come in useful. But I can tell you that I am here to protect you from dangers *as yet unknown*. Because whatever lies at the other end of that wormhole –' and here the Doctor jabbed a long finger in an apparently random direction that Clara suspected was the *exact* direction of the wormhole – 'it won't be good. In fact, it will be both deadly and monstrous.'

'What?' Balfour almost choked on his champagne.

'Rubbish,' said Marco Spritt.

'He's not a magician,' said Tanya Flexx. 'He's a lunatic!'

Clara felt awkward. The Doctor could be so embarrassing at times. 'What the Doctor means is that... well, he's very experienced in matters like this. He's met... lots of monsters.' It was lame and she finished by biting her lip to stop herself saying anything more.

'You're both lunatics,' said Tanya.

'You didn't mention anything about monsters when

you asked to join the team, Doctor,' said Balfour, sounding a little peeved. 'You told me that the wormhole was unstable. You warned me that there would be an element of danger. You didn't say anything about monsters. You just said that you were an expert in space-time travel and could act as scientific adviser to the expedition.'

'I did, yes. And it was true. I left out the bit about monsters because I didn't want to put you off.'

'What exactly are your qualifications, Doctor?' demanded Tibby Vent.

'What monsters?' asked Luis Cranmer quietly. It was the first time he'd spoken.

The Doctor's finger swung towards Cranmer. 'Ah! The first sensible question of the evening!'

Marco got to his feet. 'I'm not prepared to listen to any more of this nonsense. I'm going to bed.'

'Trugg will show you to your cabin,' said Balfour quickly.

The robot towered over Marco. 'If you'd care to follow me, sir?'

'Get on with it, then,' Marco snapped. He said a gruff goodnight to the others, glowered at the Doctor, and then followed Trugg out of the lounge.

'Marco Spritt's information is vital to the success of this mission,' Tibby sighed. She rubbed her tired eyes with one hand. 'It's taken a lot of painstaking work to match up the information he has on the *Carthage* with the Phaeron map.'

'Marco probably doesn't mean to be rude,' said Balfour generously. 'It's just that finding what happened to the *Carthage* means so much to him. It's become a sort of obsession, I think.'

'Is that so?' said the Doctor. 'How interesting.'

'Maybe it's best if we all get some sleep before we reach the wormhole.' Balfour wished them all goodnight and followed Marco out of the room.

'You still haven't explained about the monsters,' said Luis Cranmer.

'Poor old Luis,' laughed Tanya. 'He hates space travel so much. And now monsters.'

'I get space sick,' Cranmer explained. He hadn't touched his champagne and he looked a ghastly colour. He stood up shakily and said, 'In fact I think I'd better lie down. I don't feel very well.'

'If you're gonna puke, mind you don't do it outside my cabin,' advised Tanya. 'Take two of those pills I gave you and see me in the morning.'

Without another word Cranmer hurried out of the room, one hand clamped over his mouth.

'So much for the party,' Tanya said. She gulped down the last of her champagne and stood up to leave. 'I'd better hit the sack myself before it gets too wild. Call me in the morning – but not too early.' She winked at Clara and then swept out of the common room.

The Doctor and Clara were left with Tibby Vent.

'So what are these monsters you're talking about?' Tibby asked the Doctor. 'The Phaeron? I doubt they looked human, but that doesn't mean they were monsters.'

'You don't need to look like a monster to be one,' replied the Doctor.

'Maybe not. But whatever they looked like, and whatever they did, they were an extremely advanced species. They were highly civilised. Technologically speaking they were well ahead of us, long before they died out. I can't believe they were monsters.'

'I never said they were,' the Doctor said. 'But they built a vast network of intergalactic roads through hyperspace and then closed them all down in a great hurry. Why do you think that was?'

'I've no idea. But we've got the chance to find out. They left one last wormhole open, remember.'

'Yes, they did.' The Doctor met her cool gaze easily. 'Ever wonder why?'

'That's why I'm standing here.' Tibby smiled icily. 'So it's a bit late to scare me off now, wouldn't you say? Goodnight.'

And with that she brushed past the Doctor and left the room.

Clara winced. 'I hope they don't all have nightmares.'

'I hope they do,' replied the Doctor. 'It might help prepare them for what lies ahead.'

Chapter
3

'Looks like I missed quite a party,' said Dan Laker as he entered the room with his customary smile. 'Everyone all right?' He found the champagne and poured himself a glass.

'You didn't miss much,' Clara told him.

She watched the pilot as he sank down into one of the armchairs with a sigh. He looked worn out, and a little older than Clara had originally thought. This Laker appeared to be in his late forties, his handsome features just beginning to show character: rugged, determined, but with good humour behind watchful grey eyes. He raised his glass towards Clara and said, 'Cheers.'

Clara felt the need to explain. 'It was just Balfour introducing everybody. I don't know why you weren't invited.'

'I was. I just didn't come. I was busy on the flight deck and besides, I'm not one for socialising much. I prefer to do my drinking on my own.'

'Oh.' Clara glanced at his empty champagne glass. 'Do you want us to leave?'

'Nope.' Laker gave her one of his lazy smiles. 'This isn't drinking. This is celebrating.'

'Good. What are we celebrating?'

'We're approaching the wormhole,' said the Doctor as he sat down in the opposite chair. 'We should reach the transition point in hyperspace very soon. Isn't that right, Captain?'

Laker tipped his head in acknowledgement. 'How did you know?'

'Felt the change in the ion thrust as we vectored in. It's unmistakable.' The Doctor closed his eyes. 'I'd say we are about two hours from transition. Maybe less.'

'I'm impressed. Not many people are that tuned in to space travel – unless they're astrogators.'

'Like Jem, you mean.' The Doctor's eyes snapped open. 'She's physically tied to the ship, isn't she? The navigational computer matrix connects directly to her cerebral cortex.'

Clara didn't like the sound of that. 'What? Like she's actually plugged into the ship?'

The Doctor nodded. 'It's the only way to guarantee perfect cohesion between human and ship. Jem feels her way through hyperspace – and the ship uses her as its guide.'

'That doesn't sound very nice.'

'It's fine,' said Laker. 'Really. It's what Jem wants.'

'Is it?' wondered the Doctor. 'The way I see it, Jem doesn't have much choice.'

Clara glanced at the Doctor. His eyes were fierce beneath his bristling eyebrows. There was real anger there.

'I know what you're thinking, Doctor,' said Laker tiredly. 'I've heard it all before… that astrogators are just slaves—'

'Worse than slaves,' said the Doctor. 'Astrogation clones were developed by the military during the last Draconian War as a cheap and effective method of space navigation. They were genetically engineered from artificial stem cells to serve that one, single purpose – to be plugged into a spaceship as a biological component. Not humanity's finest hour.'

'It's more complicated than that,' Laker argued.

'There's nothing complicated about it at all. Astrogators can't do anything except fly spaceships and they have a very short life span. When they die, or they've been burnt out by some badly tuned computer interface, they just get replaced by another one.'

'Not Jem,' said Laker.

There was such basic sadness in the pilot's voice that even the Doctor paused.

'She's the last one left,' said Laker quietly.

The Doctor looked shocked. 'The last one?'

'I was a transport pilot during the war,' explained Laker. 'They gave me Jem as my navigator. She was good. In fact she was the best in the business. I mean she could sense other ships in hyperspace, you know?' The pilot shook his head in simple admiration. 'We flew the major supply routes between Earth Central and the Draconian Front and never got caught once. When the war ended, I left the Space Service and I took Jem with me.'

The Doctor considered this carefully. 'That must have been quite a risk.'

'I had no choice. They were decommissioning the other clones.'

'Meaning deliberate burnout?'

'I couldn't let that happen to Jem. We stole a ship and took off. That was twenty years ago and I've never been back to Earth since.'

The Doctor sat back in his chair and studied the pilot with fresh eyes. The angry stare had gone. 'That's remarkable,' he said.

'I suppose it is.' Laker's easy smile returned. 'We've been working together ever since, flying our own ships for hire on the galactic rim. It's been a successful business but we're ready to retire. I'm not getting any younger and as for Jem…'

'She's lived far longer than any other astrogation clone.'

Laker nodded. 'It's time we settled down.'

'And this job for Raymond Balfour is your nest egg?'

'Balfour is paying well. Really well. Money's no object for him – well, just look at this ship if you want proof of that. It's the best ship we've ever had, and we've had quite a few.'

'But isn't flying through this wormhole thing a big risk?' Clara asked.

'All space flying is a big risk, miss. And Balfour's making it worth our while. But the real truth of the matter is, only Jem can find this wormhole and only she can navigate it.'

'That's why you didn't come down from the flight deck,' Clara realised. 'You didn't want to leave Jem on her own.'

Laker nodded. 'She's sleeping now. The ship's on course for the wormhole and she's letting her subconscious handle things for a while.' He got to his feet. 'I'd better get back soon, anyway. I like to be there for her when she wakes up, and it won't be long before we reach the transition point.'

'It's been nice to meet you,' Clara said, getting up. 'And Jem.'

'Likewise,' said the Doctor, also standing.

Laker paused by the door. 'Oh, by the way, Doctor… that thing in the hold. Your police box.'

'The TARDIS. What about it?'

'My people were quite intrigued by it.'

The Doctor's eyes narrowed. 'Your people?'

'My engineers. Sorry, I forgot you haven't met them yet.'

'I've a feeling I'm about to.'

'They're down in the hold with your box right now. They're trying to figure out—'

But the Doctor had already turned on his heel and was running out of the lounge.

Clara was left on her own once Laker departed for the flight deck. She found herself yawning widely. She knew the Doctor seldom slept, but she had finished another long day at Coal Hill a short while ago and the champagne had gone straight to her head. A lie down felt like just the thing she needed. She wandered out of the lounge, hoping to follow the Doctor back to the TARDIS, but almost immediately she ran into Trugg.

The huge robot loomed over her, filling the corridor. Her face was reflected in the burnished metal of its torso. Lights blinked steadily on and off on its large ovoid head.

'Can I help you, miss?' Trugg's voice was simultaneously comforting and ever so slightly threatening. But perhaps being eight feet tall and made from half a ton of steel just made it seem that way.

Clara was about to ask for directions to the hold when she found herself yawning again. She covered her mouth and forced her eyes open wide to look more awake. 'Oh dear,' she said eventually. 'Excuse me. More tired than I thought.'

'Would you like me to show you to your cabin?' asked Trugg.

'I have a cabin?'

'Everyone has a cabin. Mr Balfour was most insistent when the ship was designed that there should be room for all aboard to be housed comfortably.'

Clara was tempted. It couldn't hurt to just check it out, anyway. 'OK,' she said. 'Thanks.'

'This way, miss.' Trugg pivoted with a whine of motorised joints and set off along the corridor. It curved around what Clara thought must be the circumference of the ship. 'Your cabin is located on the starboard side, room number 7.'

Almost immediately Clara heard someone talking further along the corridor. It was Marco Spritt's voice. She couldn't see him yet because of the curve but she could hear him well enough.

'I just thought you'd want a bit of company,' he was saying. There was a strange, insistent tone in his voice that Clara didn't like.

There was no reply, and, curious, Clara slowed down so

that she didn't walk straight into view. Interestingly, Trugg also halted, as if waiting for her signal to continue.

'What's wrong with a bit of company?' Marco continued. 'Everyone likes a nightcap.'

This was followed by the sound of knocking on a door. It wasn't loud, but there was an urgency to it.

'Come on,' Marco said. 'Open the door. Just for a while. We can get to know each other a little better, can't we?'

Clara had heard enough, and she walked on until she saw Marco standing outside one of the cabin doors. He had a bottle of wine in one hand.

'What's up?' Clara asked. 'Can't find your cabin?'

'None of your business, actually,' Marco replied. He looked Clara up and down and then looked at Trugg, who towered over them both.

'This is Professor Vent's cabin,' said Trugg.

'Get lost, robot,' said Marco. 'I'm busy. Go on, move along. Nothing to see here.'

'Perhaps you would like me to direct you to your own cabin, sir?'

Marco snorted. 'No thanks, I'm fine.'

'Might be for the best,' Clara said. 'Maybe Tibby doesn't fancy a nightcap, after all.'

'What would you know about it?' Marco replied. He sighed. 'Look, your Doctor pal really scared Tibby with all that stupid talk about monsters. I just wanted to check she was OK.'

'With a bottle of wine?'

Marco shrugged. 'I couldn't think of anything else. It's an excuse. I just want to make sure she's all right, that's all.'

Clara knocked on the door. 'Tibby? It's Clara. You OK in there?'

There was a pause and then Tibby's voice could be heard on the other side of the door. 'Yes. I'm fine. I just want to go to bed.'

'I think that's clear enough, don't you?' Clara asked Marco. It wasn't lost on him that Clara was speaking with the benefit of an eight-foot robot standing right behind her.

He scowled at them both. 'Whatever,' he muttered, and stomped off down the corridor.

Clara waited until he had disappeared from view then knocked on Tibby's door again. 'Tibby? He's gone. Relax.'

The door opened, and Tibby said, 'Thanks. Come in.'

The cabin had a single bunk, a wardrobe and a desk unit. There were books and datapads and various other scholarly items on every surface. A 3D holographic map of the galaxy was floating in the air above the desk. There were little dots of red light all over it.

'What are they?' Clara asked.

'The wormholes,' Tibby said, picking up a remote control. 'Or rather where the wormholes used to be. This is a computer simulation of the Phaeron map from Ganymede. And this here…' She zoomed in on a tiny point of red light flashing in the air, about a foot away from the edge of the galactic disc. 'This is our wormhole. The last Phaeron Road.'

'That's where we're headed?'

'Yup.' Tibby stifled a yawn. 'Sorry. I should sound more excited. But the truth is I'm shattered. I was on Ursa Minor when I got the call from Balfour: the ship was ready, the crew was ready, we had clearance... I had to drop everything and get to Far Station.'

Clara nodded sympathetically. She knew how that felt.

'It's been a long time in planning, but the last few days have been a whirlwind,' sighed Tibby.

'And Marco?'

'We needed his knowledge of the *Carthage* to help pinpoint the exact location of that.' Tibby touched the little red light blinking in mid-air.

'But you wish he wasn't here?'

'Balfour doesn't know what Marco's really like. He thinks the best of everybody.'

Clara smiled. 'I think Balfour might be a bit of a romantic at heart.'

'Yeah. And Marco – well, he's got another kind of romance in mind. One that I'm not interested in.' Tibby switched off the galaxy hologram and threw the remote control down. 'It's just me and the Phaeron. It always has been.'

'I'll ask Trugg to keep an eye on Marco,' said Clara, getting up to leave.

Tibby smiled at her. 'Thanks. And thanks for heading him off.'

'No problem. I had help – in fact, Trugg's probably still waiting outside.'

'Well, good night, then,' Tibby said. 'See you later.'

Clara let herself out and sure enough, the giant robot was still waiting. He showed Clara to cabin number 7 and then she thanked him.

'I'm just doing my job, miss.'

'No, I mean with Marco. It was good that you were there.'

'I didn't do anything, miss.'

'Oh, you did, Trugg. You did.'

'Well, I dunno what the hell it is,' said Mitch Keller.

The *Alexandria* didn't have a hold as such because it wasn't a cargo vessel, but it did have a wide storage bay on the base deck with a high ceiling. Standing right in the middle of it was a tall blue box with a lamp on its roof and little frosted-glass windows set into tall, narrow doors.

'It's a police box,' said Hobbo. 'Says so, don't it?'

Mitch walked around the police box once more. He was old and rangy, with a white beard and careful eyes. He was wearing faded spacer's overalls and an old baseball cap with 'I ♥ Mars' on it. Hobbo wasn't wrong; there was a panel at the top of the box on all four sides that proclaimed 'POLICE PUBLIC CALL BOX'.

'I just don't get it,' he muttered. 'I signed everything on board this ship. There was nothin' on the manifest about a police box.'

Hobbo was sitting on a packing crate nursing a hot drink. She looked bored. She wore an old hoody over her fatigues and a heavy tool belt. 'Give it a rest, Mitch,' she said. 'Just cos there's nothin' else to do round here doesn't mean you've gotta go lookin' for problems.' She tilted her head to one side and eyed the police box. 'Who cares what it is, anyways? Probably something Balfour wanted on voyage. He's stupid rich; who knows what's going on in his head?'

Mitch reached out and touched the box. 'It's humming,' he said. 'You can feel it. Like there's machinery inside.'

'Maybe he keeps a spare service robot in there.'

'What would be the point of that?' Mitch took off his cap and scratched his head. He didn't need any puzzles or worries now, not at his age, but there was something damned strange about this box. The fact that it was locked was really bugging him too. He gave the door handle an experimental tug but it was no use. 'I just don't get it. It's—'

'Incongruous,' said the Doctor, stepping between Mitch and the TARDIS. 'That's what it is.'

Mitch jerked back. 'Who the hell—'

'I'm the Doctor. You must be…?'

'Mitch Keller, chief engineer.' Mitch found himself responding automatically. 'This is Harley Hobson, my assistant. Everyone calls her Hobbo.'

'Who said you could poke around my TARDIS?' asked the Doctor, his eyebrows bristling ferociously.

'TARDIS?'

'It's mine,' said the Doctor, patting the police box. 'It makes a mockery of space and transcends time itself. Completely out of your league.'

'Yeah,' Mitch agreed. He pulled his cap back on. 'Wait a sec. Just wait a damn sec. This is yours? How the hell did you get it on board?'

'I thought I just explained that: space, mockery, transcends time.'

Hobbo was chuckling to herself. 'You had to ask, Mitch…'

'Sorry it took me so long to get here,' the Doctor said.

'I got distracted on the way. Had a quick look round your engine room…'

Hobbo's smile faded instantly. 'What? Who said you could go poking around in—'

'Touché,' said the Doctor. 'Anyway, it's all shipshape and in good order.'

'The *Alexandria* is fresh out of the box,' grumbled Hobbo.

'In that case the megaton valves are probably too tight. Try loosening them a bit.'

'I knew there was something,' Mitch said. He looked at the Doctor with respect. 'This ship's sweet as a nut but there was *somethin'* about those meg valves…'

'There's nothin' wrong with 'em,' Hobbo insisted. She jumped down from the crate, her face crumpling into a petulant frown. 'There's nothin' wrong with *anythin'* on this crate. There's so much not wrong with it there's nothin' to do.'

'Just check them, will you, Hobbo?' asked Mitch. 'Try loosenin' them, like the man says. See if he's right.'

'Loosen the megaton valves?' Hobbo looked disgusted. 'That's gonna take all night.'

'Just do it,' Mitch said as Hobbo opened her mouth to argue. He was easy-going by nature but there was a certain tone of voice he used when he was giving what amounted to an order.

'Here, let me take that,' the Doctor offered, taking Hobbo's still steaming mug. He sniffed appreciatively. 'Is that hot chocolate?'

'Knock yourself out,' Hobbo replied as she sauntered out.

Mitch turned to the Doctor with a smile. 'She ain't happy unless she's complainin',' he said.

'I like her already,' said the Doctor, sipping the hot chocolate.

Marco Spritt lay on his bunk, fully dressed. He was fuming. The cabin was in complete disarray; clothes and equipment strewn around where he'd hurled it all in a fit of temper as soon as he closed the door.

He was staring at the datapad Balfour had handed out in the common room. It showed a picture of Tabitha Vent. It must have been an old publicity photo because she looked a lot younger than she did now. Marco flung the datapad across the room with a curse. He'd have been with Tibby now if it wasn't for the Oswald woman interfering. He didn't like her at all. She was too bossy, too prim, too much like a teacher and Marco had *hated* school. He'd done well for himself despite school. He'd done it all himself, on his own, without help, and he would carry on doing things that way.

He opened up a 3D schematic of the *Carthage* on his personal computer and flicked through the images of the engines, the cabins, the flight decks and stasis tanks. They were more familiar to him than any other spacecraft in existence.

His mother had tried to tell him what to do as well, usually at long range – via interstellar hypernet messages that were delayed by months, or sometimes even years. She'd left him on his own at school to fend for himself. Marco liked to think there would be a reckoning when he found her. There'd be a reckoning with Clara Oswald too, if he had his way. And that cadaverous Doctor.

Marco switched off the computer and wondered what the Doctor and Clara were really doing on the *Alexandria*. There was something odd about them, about the way they'd just turned up out of the blue like that. He brooded on it for several minutes and then, abruptly, got up from his bunk and left his cabin.

Chapter

4

Dan Laker walked back onto the flight deck and listened carefully. It was wonderfully quiet. Even on luxury starliners you could hear the engines, but the *Alexandria* just purred through space, cat-silent. The instruments guided the vessel with a calm assurance. The ship hardly needed a pilot. Laker had never felt more like a passenger in his life. The only important person on the flight deck now was Jem.

She lay quietly, hardly breathing. Her eyes were open, but Laker knew she was not fully conscious. It was said that astrogator clones were never truly alive unless they were dreaming, and thus at one with the cosmos.

After a few minutes, the holographic indicators on the couch terminals showed Jem's heart rate and blood pressure were beginning to increase, which meant she was close to waking again. Laker glanced at the holoviewer. It was as black as a shark's eye; nothing but intergalactic space.

Jem stirred. Her eyes flickered and widened as consciousness returned and she sucked in a sudden, shaking breath.

Laker felt a pang of concern. 'Hey, are you OK?'

She smiled. 'Yes, I think so. Just tired, that's all.'

'Just keep thinking of Chasima Orion and a villa overlooking the Sand Sea.'

'Sunlight from a binary star,' said Jem dreamily.

'It'll be warm and peaceful, and there'll be no one there but us. I've had the villa kitted out with exactly what you need.'

Jem's hand reached out for his. 'I only need you.'

Her hand was soft and pale, tiny in his. He held it as tightly as he dared. 'How's it going?'

'We are close to the Phaeron Road.'

Laker looked at the holoviewer, but there was only blackness out there.

'You won't be able to see it,' Jem said. 'Not yet – not until we're right on top of it and ready to enter. But I can sense it. I can feel the way space is bending towards it.' She closed her eyes and, from nothing, a frown appeared.

'What's the matter?'

'Ripples,' she said quietly. 'Striations in the dark matter around us.'

Laker rarely understood exactly what Jem meant when she talked like this, but he was always alert to how it made her feel: calm, or happy, or fulfilled. But now she seemed perturbed by something.

'It's like a whisper in space,' she said. 'Telling me something – something I can't quite hear.'

Laker was frustrated. 'Is it important?'

'Everything is important, Dan.' She settled back in her

couch and her eyes glazed over. 'We're getting closer. The whisper is getting louder.'

'I'd better call the others,' Laker said. 'Balfour will want to see this and—'

'No,' said Jem softly. 'Leave it for a moment. Let's enjoy this for ourselves, just for a moment. Think of Chasima Orion.'

'OK,' Laker said. He squeezed her hand and looked at the holoviewer again. Somewhere out there was the transition point between normal space and the wormhole, but no matter how hard he looked, Laker could only see darkness.

Clara opened her eyes when she heard the knock at her door. She'd actually drifted off. The room wasn't huge but it was warm and comfortable, with a bunk and a closet and a place to store clothes. It felt like a hotel. She'd lain down on the bed and closed her eyes and the warmth and the champagne and the long day at school had done the rest.

'Hang on,' she said, sitting up and pressing the door control.

The cabin door hissed open, and the Doctor came in. He had a mug in each hand. 'Thought you might like some hot chocolate. It'll help you sleep.'

'Believe me, I don't need any help there.' Clara took the drink anyway and sniffed it and sipped. 'Hm. That's good. I didn't think they'd have hot chocolate here.'

The Doctor frowned. 'Why not?'

'Because, you know, in the future and everything.' Clara raised the mug with a smile. 'Hot chocolate – who knew?'

'Well, it's not actually hot chocolate. It's purely synthetic, made by the ship's drinks machine from recycled waste products.'

Clara gagged. 'Waste products?'

'Well, something's got to be done with all the human excreta. What do you want them to do – just eject it into space? I thought Coal Hill School was keen on recycling.'

Clara was staring at the mug in her hand. 'Even so…'

'It's just a case of mixing the right flavours, anyway,' the Doctor explained happily. 'Like colours. Only in this case you just take all the right chemical ingredients from the waste and mix it together to make hot chocolate. Or something that tastes just like it. It all comes down to chemistry in the end, Clara. It was quite fun experimenting, actually.'

'Experimenting?'

'Well I had to make a few adjustments to the drinks machine. And I used a cup of genuine hot chocolate as a control.' He raised his own mug and took a sip, smacking his lips with relish.

'You've got real hot chocolate, then?'

'Well, of course. No point in me trying the synthetic stuff – I knew which was which so it wouldn't be a true test.'

'So I'm just drinking this recycled… stuff… as a test?'

The Doctor nodded eagerly. 'Does it pass? Tell me the truth.'

'It's… hot.' Clara put the mug down on the little table by the bunk. 'I'll let it cool for a bit.'

'Good idea.'

'Doctor… why are we really here? I don't like the sound

of this wormhole thing, and I can't believe you've brought us here just to meet the worm that made it.'

'Oh no, I wouldn't advise meeting a Space Worm. Most human brains can't cope with them. It would be highly irresponsible of me to introduce you to a Space Worm. But this wormhole wasn't made by any kind of a worm. It was manufactured.'

'By the Phaeron?'

The Doctor nodded thoughtfully. 'Beings of great power and massively advanced technology. They practically ran this part of the universe, billions of years ago, criss-crossing the galaxies with their hyperspace conduits.'

'The Phaeron Roads? Do you know much about them?'

'Not really. It's an era I've never visited. It's taken me nearly 2,000 years to just scratch the surface of time and space, Clara. I can't know everything. But I do know there's hardly anything left of them in this time period. Professor Grumpy was very lucky to find the relics she did. That archaeological dig on Ganymede was exceptionally fortunate.'

Clara caught the Doctor's tone immediately. 'Too exceptional?'

The Doctor pulled a face and shrugged.

'Come on.' Clara nudged him with her elbow. 'There's something you're not telling me.'

The Doctor blew out a deep breath. 'According to some legends, the Phaeron were forced to shut down their wormholes by the Time Lords.'

'Your people?'

'Long before my time. Long before your galaxy was

fully formed. In those darker days, the Time Lords weren't so averse to interfering in the affairs of the universe. It's possible they saw the Phaeron as a threat. Or perhaps the Phaeron had discovered something the Time Lords wanted kept hidden. Either way, they closed down the roads and left the Phaeron to rot.'

'That seems harsh.'

'It was. Without the roads the Phaeron couldn't function properly. Their once fruitful civilisation withered on the vine.'

'Except for this one last wormhole, right?'

'The last Phaeron Road.'

'Why didn't the Time Lords shut it down with the others?'

'Because it was hidden. It was a secret road, Clara. Unknown to anyone except the Phaeron.'

'What was it then? A bolthole? Somewhere they could hide until the Time Lords went away?'

'Perhaps.'

Clara sat forward, intrigued. 'What then? Come on, out with it. I can tell that look – like you've swallowed a wasp.'

The Doctor grimaced. 'Actually, I think I might have got the hot chocolates the wrong way round.'

Clara took the Doctor's mug and sniffed it. She pulled a face. 'You're right.'

'Mixing flavours is harder than it looks.'

'I imagine it depends what flavours you're starting with. Anyway. Go on. The Phaerons' last road. Where does it lead?'

'The truth?' The Doctor stared into space. The intensity

of that stare frightened Clara sometimes. It was almost as if the Doctor could see through the spaceship walls and out into space. 'I don't know. I doubt it leads to the Andromeda galaxy. But the Phaeron are only part of the problem here.'

'There's something else?'

'It's just a rumour. Little more than a legend, in fact. One of those tales that go hand in hand with ancient, lost civilisations… but nevertheless make too much sense to ignore.'

Clara shivered. The Doctor's expression was grave, almost as if he was being forced to tread on ground he knew to be unsafe, like a man with no choice but to walk across a minefield.

'You may or may not recall something called the Glamour, Clara. It's difficult to know because by its very nature it affects people's perceptions, often in different ways…'

'The Glamour?' Clara frowned. 'Yeah, I remember that. It makes itself into whatever you most desire. It can be anything.'

'Indeed. But the Glamour is more than just a bundle of charisma. Its powers of attraction and attention can be malignant. You saw what it did to Lancelot's knights. That's why it likes to hide. But shapeshifting is only part of its repertoire of tricks. The fact is no one knows the exact extent of its powers or influence. Is it an artefact? A living thing? Is it sentient? Everyone perceives it in a different way, everyone reacts to it in a different way… and the Glamour feeds off the emotions it provokes. It soaks up desire and revels in jealousy. But it's very hard to find – and that's part of its deadly allure.' The Doctor gave a sad, rueful laugh. 'You always want what you can't have.'

'So what's this got to do with the Phaeron and the wormhole?'

'The Glamour has been lost for centuries now – thank goodness. But the rumour I heard tied the very origins of the Glamour to the Phaeron.'

Clara sat up. 'You mean they invented it?'

'I'm not sure. But they certainly took it to the grave with them.'

'I don't understand.'

'I think the Glamour is why the Time Lords closed the Phaeron Roads, Clara.'

'You mean they caused an entire race to go extinct just to get rid of the Glamour?'

The Doctor gave an exaggerated shrug. 'Who knows? I don't. But if they did… and this last Phaeron wormhole has been left open deliberately…'

'Then there's a way for the Glamour to get out?'

'With a little help, yes.'

'Help? Who would want to help?'

'Your guess is as good as mine. But we're currently on board a spaceship heading into the last Phaeron wormhole.'

Clara felt distinctly uncomfortable. 'So you mean someone on this ship might be under the influence of the Glamour?'

'Everyone wants something, Clara.'

Clara thought back. It was easy to see what Professor

Vent wanted – to meet the Phaeron, or what remained of them. Marco Spritt wanted the *Carthage* and his mother. Dan Laker wanted… what? A retirement package for him and Jem? And what about Luis Cranmer or Tanya Flexx – what did they want? Or even Raymond Balfour? He couldn't possibly want anything – he was rich enough to get everything he wanted. None of them sounded like victims of a mysterious, magnetic power. It was all very confusing.

'We don't really know enough about them to be sure, do we?' she asked.

'Perhaps things will become more apparent as we go on.'

She searched his face for a clue as to whether he really had a plan or not. 'Maybe we should get to know them better,' she suggested.

'Best not to get too attached, Clara…'

'What does that mean?' She glared at him. 'Because it's dangerous? Because they might die?'

'We have to tread very carefully now.'

'I don't think I like what you're implying. I don't want to just… watch and wait to see who's under the influence of this Glamour thing. I want to help them. I want to warn them, to stop them…'

She stood up abruptly, full of urgency, but the Doctor's hand shot out and grasped her wrist. His eyes bored into hers. 'You want, you want… Listen to yourself, Clara.'

'What?'

'The Glamour is the very definition of *wanting*. It will become exactly what you look for, what you most desire.

And the closer you get to it the more it will attract you and exert its power over you. It will hold you in its thrall and suck you dry.'

Slowly Clara sat back down on the bunk. She was more confused than ever. 'So what do we do?'

'Well—'

In the space of a heartbeat Clara was sent sprawling across the cabin as the ship lurched suddenly to one side. 'What the hell was that?'

But the Doctor had already sprung across the cabin and darted out of the door. He nearly ran straight into Marco Spritt, who was looking equally surprised.

'What's happening?' Marco demanded.

The Doctor brushed past him without a word. Clara wondered for a moment what Marco had been doing right outside her cabin but then forgot about it as the *Alexandria* shook violently, pitching them both from one side of the corridor to the other. Shouts came from various cabins and Clara saw Tanya Flexx's tousled head appear from an open doorway.

'Who's rocking the boat?' she yelled.

Another door opened, and Luis Cranmer tumbled out. 'What's going on?'

There was a loud, mechanical screech from deep below decks that Clara guessed could only be bad news. The *Alexandria* gave another bone-rattling shudder and the Doctor glanced back at her, his eyes wide with fear. 'Astronic overload,' he shouted. 'The ship's tearing itself apart!'

Chapter

5

Alarm lights flashed on the *Alexandria*'s flight deck and a warning klaxon filled the room with noise. The Doctor crossed to a bank of controls and stopped the klaxon as Clara followed him onto the flight deck, still struggling to keep her balance. Behind her came Marco and Tanya in rapid succession. They were all demanding to know what was going on.

'Everybody sit down and shut up,' the Doctor said firmly.

'What's happening?' asked Raymond Balfour, staggering onto the flight deck.

'Including you,' the Doctor said. 'Shut up.'

'Hey!' Balfour stared at him. The millionaire was wearing an elaborately patterned silk dressing gown and, like the others, had clearly rushed out of his cabin at the first sign of trouble. Trugg was with him. The robot took up a huge amount of space and towered menacingly over the Doctor. 'You can't speak to me like that! Trugg! Tell him he can't speak to me like that!'

'I'm afraid he just did, sir,' said the robot.

'Listen, if there's any kind of emergency then the Doctor can probably help,' Clara said in what she hoped was a calming and reasonable tone of voice.

'*If?*' echoed Balfour as warning lights around the flight deck continued to flash.

'What the blue blazes is going on?' demanded Tabitha Vent as she too came in. Behind her was Luis Cranmer, looking bewildered and frightened. Within the space of a few seconds the flight deck had become crowded.

The Doctor had joined Dan Laker by the astrogation couch, where Jem 428 was twisting and turning like someone caught in a nightmare. The hologram displays fizzed and jerked in the air around her.

'What happened?' the Doctor asked.

'I've no idea,' Laker said, his voice shaky. 'One minute everything was fine – then she had some sort of seizure and started talking about voices in space. Next thing the ship went haywire.'

Clara pointed at the main holoviewer. Something was glittering at its centre, sending random shards of light flickering outwards. 'What's that?'

'The wormhole,' said the Doctor.

'We weren't supposed to reach the transition point for another ten minutes,' said Laker.

'The coordinates where the *Carthage* disappeared were approximate,' Marco pointed out. 'They matched the Phaeron map location but there had to be some room for error.'

'No one's blaming you, Spritt,' growled Laker. 'I just don't know what's happened. Neither does Jem.'

Jem's eyes were wide open and her breath was coming in ragged gasps. The Doctor examined her quickly, checking her pulse and the connections to her augmentation ports. Saliva was gathering at the corners of her mouth as she struggled to speak.

'She's fitting,' Tanya said, moving closer.

Clara had seen a boy suffer an epileptic attack at school; she remembered only too well how helpless she had felt then, and now was no different.

Laker was ashen. 'I've never seen her like this before. What should I do?'

'Hold the ship as steady as you can,' the Doctor told him, and the pilot nodded, backing slowly away to take the captain's chair.

Clara glanced at the hologram viewer again and saw a shimmering nexus of energy growing larger by the second. They were hurtling towards it.

Jem reached up and grasped the Doctor's arm, white fingers digging into the dark material of his jacket. 'I can hear whispers in the dark, like nothing I've ever heard before. Warning us. Telling us not to go on…'

'We should abort,' Laker said.

'No!' Marco protested. 'We can't! We mustn't! Balfour, tell him! Tell him we can't abort!'

'You heard what Jem said!' Laker began to operate the flight controls manually. 'I'm turning us around.'

'Stay on course!' screamed Marco.

'It's the imperfection,' Jem gasped. 'The imperfection…'

'What's she talking about?' asked Clara.

'I've no idea,' the Doctor said. 'Something imprinted in

the exotic matter of the wormhole perhaps, picked up by her etheric sub-senses…'

'I don't understand a word you're saying, Doctor,' said Laker through gritted teeth.

'It doesn't matter,' insisted Marco. 'Just keep going.'

'He's right.' Jem looked at Laker, imploring him. 'Don't stop. Think of Chasima Orion!'

Laker's hands froze on the controls. 'But…'

'We can't stop now,' Jem said. 'We must go on.'

As usual, Clara found herself looking to the Doctor for advice, for confirmation, for leadership. But this time his expression was unreadable, his face stony, his eyes inscrutable. 'Doctor?' she prompted,

'I don't think we have any choice,' he replied.

The ship shook again, deep into its core, and suddenly controls panels all around the flight deck exploded in bright showers of sparks. The holoviewer was alive with an unearthly radiance. Streaks of flickering, silvery light raced out from the centre of the hologram, increasing in speed and ferocity until there was nothing but an insane, strobing pattern and at the centre of this a tiny dot of blackness appeared.

Clara watched, mesmerised, as the black dot grew into a ball of dark matter. Light swirled across the surface, which was the deepest, glossiest black she had ever seen. Everything was reflected and distorted, as if the ball was a perfect, mirrored sphere.

'The last road of the Phaeron,' said Jem breathlessly.

'Why's it round like a ball?' asked Clara.

'It's not,' said the Doctor. 'The transition point of a

wormhole is a four-dimensional object, but the screen interprets images in three dimensions – and the best it can do is a sphere.'

The ball grew larger until it filled the screen. A strange silver shape appeared at its centre; Clara wondered if it was the reflection of the *Alexandria*. She thought she could see colours now, swirling across the surface, as darkly iridescent as oil on water.

The *Alexandria* had stopped its violent shaking, but there was a deep, insistent vibration running through the vessel. Occasional groans and creaks echoed through the ship as the superstructure reacted to unusual pressures.

'Steady as she goes, Captain Laker,' said the Doctor.

The glimmering darkness filled the screen. Brilliantly swirling colours bled away until the flight deck was once more in shadow.

Clara reached out and grabbed the Doctor's arm, just to make sure he was still there. The brief flashes from electrical short circuits created snapshot visions of the people around her: Jem's white face, painfully drawn; Laker watching her anxiously; Tanya rooted to the spot, apparently out of her depth; Tibby Vent and Balfour holding on to each other for support.

A terrible scream filled the flight deck, causing everyone to flinch. Laker was out of his seat in an instant and at Jem's side. 'What's wrong? What's happening to her?'

'She's having another seizure,' said Tanya.

'She's never screamed like that before.'

'Well she's screaming like that now.'

The Doctor grabbed Jem's wrists and held them fast. Her

eyes bulged and there was foam on her lips as she threw her head from side to side. The *Alexandria* also rocked from side to side, the engines howling.

Clara clutched the astrogation couch. 'Is she going to be all right?'

Jem's back arched wildly and a horrible, coughing gasp blew out of her mouth as if she was trying to clear a blockage from her throat. Her eyes were round and protruding as she turned to look at Dan Laker. There was nothing in her eyes now but fear and pain and the ship was shaking uncontrollably.

The Doctor glanced at Laker. 'We have to disconnect her from the ship.'

'We can't do that,' said Tanya. 'She's flying the ship straight through a wormhole. Unhooking her now could kill her.'

'She's locked in some sort of telepathic fugue state and it's tearing the ship apart!'

'I don't want to lose her!' protested Laker.

'I know it's a risk – but what choice do we have?'

The *Alexandria* was shaking madly now. More warning lights flashed on every control panel and alarms sprang into life all over the flight deck.

'For god's sake just get her out of there, before we all die!' yelled Marco Spritt.

'You've changed your tune!' Laker bared his teeth at him but then turned back to the Doctor and shook his head. 'I can't, Doctor! It'll kill her.'

The Doctor held his gaze. 'Marco is an unspeakable idiot but he's got a point. If we don't disconnect her now, the ship will be destroyed and we will *all* die.'

Laker looked at Jem, aghast. Her face was contorted in pain, and the entire ship was starting to groan in sympathy.

The Doctor gripped him by the arm. 'If I take some of the telepathic strain,' he said, 'it might increase her chance of survival.'

'It's too risky, Doctor,' Tanya said.

Clara looked hard at the Doctor. 'Wouldn't that be dangerous for you, too?'

'What choice do we have?' he replied.

The ship bucked wildly and sparks flew from several control panels. The hologram displays zigzagged insanely around the astrogation couch as a hot burning smell filled the flight deck and fresh alarms rang out.

The Doctor turned to Laker. 'It's now or never, Captain!'

Laker screwed his eyes shut and gave a mute nod.

The Doctor moved instantly. He placed the tips of his fingers around Jem's face and closed his eyes. His lips moved silently and his eyebrows drew together in a knot of concentration. Suddenly Jem seemed to sag lifelessly into the couch, her arms flopping loose on either side.

'Do it now,' hissed the Doctor.

Tanya began to disconnect the wires connecting the astrogation couch to the sockets in Jem's head. She moaned every time one came free, the Doctor flinching in unison. One by one the fizzing holograms winked out of existence until there were none left at all.

Then there was a sudden, unnerving movement, like a lift dropping straight down a shaft, and an intense blackness filled Clara's vision. It felt as if her eyes had simply been switched off and for a second she panicked, thinking she'd gone blind. Then she saw the faint glow of the control consoles all the others looking around in horrified relief and knew they had experienced exactly the same sensation. Finally, the *Alexandria* settled and the engines stopped their screaming.

'That's it,' Tanya said at last. 'Pulse is weak and she's barely breathing, but at least she's alive.'

The Doctor gasped as if he was coming up for air after a long swim underwater. He looked even more gaunt than usual, with deep shadows under his eyes and creases all over his face like a crumpled paper bag.

Clara helped him up. He suddenly seemed old and frail. 'Doctor! Are you all right?'

His normally bright eyes struggled to focus on Clara. 'Never… felt… better… Sarah.'

'Sarah?'

'I mean Clara. It is Clara Oswald, isn't it? You look terrible, by the way.'

'Hey, you don't look so hot yourself.'

'I'm 2,000 years old and my brain's just absorbed a huge dose of psychic feedback. What's your excuse?' The Doctor suddenly held a finger to his lips. 'Shh! Never mind. Listen.'

'I can't hear anything,' said Clara.

'Exactly.'

An eerie silence had fallen all over the ship. Laker checked more of his controls. 'The engines are dead. We've lost all motive power.'

'Look,' said Tibby, pointing at the holoviewer.

All the screen showed was a deep, impenetrable blackness that seemed to flood in and fill up the space around them. The only illumination came from the blinking console panels and monitors.

'We've left the wormhole,' said Laker.

Luis Cranmer was checking an instrument panel. 'It's gone – the wormhole has collapsed!'

They all looked at the holoviewer again and saw only darkness.

'There's nothing out there,' Tibby said, her voice strangely hollow. 'Absolutely nothing.'

'Will someone *please* tell me what's going on?' asked Raymond Balfour.

'We're adrift in deep space between the galaxies,' the Doctor said. 'Like a mote of dust floating in the dark.'

'Adrift is right,' said an old, rangy man in overalls and a baseball cap who had just walked onto the flight deck. He stopped in his tracks when he realised the room was full of people and they had all turned to look at him.

'Everyone, this is Mitch Keller, my chief engineer,' said Laker. 'If he's left the engine room and come up here then things must be bad. Let's hear it, Mitch.'

Mitch pushed the cap back on his head. 'Well, I dunno what the hell happened just now but the hyperdrive is shot to bits. Hobbo's doin' her nut.'

'What does that mean, for goodness' sake?' asked Marco impatiently.

'It means no engines,' Mitch replied. 'We're dead in the water.'

'Dead in the water?'

'It's an old seafaring expression,' said the Doctor calmly. 'It means no wind in the sails; no way to move. The ship is at the mercy of the ocean.'

Balfour stepped forward. 'Mr Keller – if you can find any way at all to get the *Alexandria* moving, there'll be a substantial bonus in it for you.'

'I guess I can save you some money, then,' said Mitch. 'Cos this baby's going nowhere, no matter how much money you throw at it.'

'But there must be something you can do!' Marco Spritt said eventually. There was an edge of panic in his voice. 'For all our sakes!'

Mitch gave him a sour look. 'You think I like being stranded out here with you?'

'Are we really stranded, Mr Keller?' asked Tibby.

'I'm sorry, miss,' said Mitch. He took off his cap and held it awkwardly in both hands. 'I don't mean to distress you.'

'You're distressing us all,' said Marco hotly. 'Money or no money, the ship's engines and function is your responsibility, Keller. I suggest you get on with it.'

'All right, Spritt, that's enough,' snapped Laker. 'I give the orders round here, not you.'

Marco folded his arms and looked away. Mitch glared at him for a few seconds longer and then sat down heavily in one of the seats. 'No point in givin' any orders if we don't have any engines.'

'I just don't understand it,' Balfour said. He looked genuinely confused. 'I bought the best ship, the best crew, the best engineers… I don't understand how it could go wrong.'

'Perhaps you forgot to buy the best of luck,' said the Doctor.

Balfour looked up sharply. 'What do you mean by that?'

'You can own the galaxy's biggest fortune, but still not be fortunate.' The Doctor thought for a moment and then, turning to Clara, said, 'I should write that one down.'

'You don't seem particularly bothered that we've lost all engine power,' Balfour noted.

The Doctor looked puzzled. 'No, I'm not bothered by that. I can fix that easy-peasy.'

'Well what are you waiting for?' interrupted Marco. 'Get on with it, man!'

The Doctor gave him an icy glare. He pointed at the holoviewer, which still showed nothing but a deep and unending blackness. 'Look out there. Nothing but vacuum and dark matter in every direction. At a rough guess I'd say we were halfway between Earth's galaxy and the next. That's about one and a quarter million light years of empty space *that* way – and one and a quarter million light years of empty space *that* way. Even if we had engine power it would take us years to get home.'

Clara swallowed. 'You mean it's like being stuck in a rowing boat in the middle of the ocean. With no oars.'

'But if the engines can be fixed,' Marco said, 'surely we could just turn around and head back through the wormhole...'

'The wormhole has collapsed,' said the Doctor. 'That's why we've ended up here, in the middle of nowhere.'

Silence fell across the flight deck.

'I'm sorry,' said the Doctor, 'but engines or no engines, there is no way back.'

Chapter

6

Clara took a deep breath and forced a smile onto her face. It was time for some positive thinking. 'Right then,' she started brightly. 'This isn't a problem; it's a challenge. What do we do next?'

'We think,' said the Doctor. 'Question: why did the wormhole collapse?'

Blank faces stared back at him.

'I'm not about to deliver a punchline,' he warned. 'I want the answer.'

'Jem said something about an *imperfection*,' Clara said. 'Could that be anything to do with it?'

'You did say the wormhole was manufactured rather than natural,' said Luis Cranmer. 'Maybe it was just too old – imperfect.'

'You mean the negative energy density could have dissipated over time?'

The Doctor began to stalk around the flight deck.

'Yes, that's possible, even likely, given the state of the exotic matter it contains, but if that was the case our entry into such a fragile wormhole would have triggered the collapse almost instantly. It brought us this far, though. Why?'

'Maybe it had done its job?' Clara asked.

'Yes,' agreed the Doctor. 'Exactly what I was thinking. The wormhole had served its purpose – which was to bring us here.'

'You mean we're supposed to be floatin' in the middle of nowhere?' asked Mitch.

'Nowhere's nowhere. Wherever we are, we're definitely *somewhere*.'

'Somewhere specific,' realised Laker. 'If the Doctor's right, then we're here for a reason. Let's find it.'

There was a gleam of satisfaction in the Doctor's eyes. Clara wondered if he wore the same look when she occasionally tumbled onto what he was already thinking. It was probably the same look she had when one of her pupils gave the right answer in a comprehension exercise.

Tibby Vent held up a computer pad. 'Let me tap into the ship's navigation matrix. If we run a search-and-match program with our last known location on the Phaeron map, we might be able to work out where we are.'

'Good idea,' said Laker, as she joined him at the flight controls. 'I'd be glad of the help.'

'Gives you a warm feeling inside, doesn't it?' said the Doctor.

'Watching people mucking in and working together?' Clara nodded. She saw it a lot in the classroom in group exercises. It was a great feeling. But there was always one, like Marco Spritt, who didn't want to join in with anything.

He stood to one side of the flight deck, scowling at the others.

'I was talking about porridge,' the Doctor said. 'I don't know about you lot but I'm starving.'

Clara looked at him. 'Porridge? Seriously?'

'No sugar on mine,' the Doctor said. 'Just a wee pinch of salt.'

'I'm not making you breakfast. I'm not your mum.'

'I made you hot chocolate.'

'Well, yeah… out of recycled… things and stuff.'

'Well I doubt Balfour's got a sack of oats just waiting in the stores. Of course you'll have to use the food machine. It's the only way of getting anything to eat on this ship, remember. It's all recycled. Trugg can help you.'

The robot whirred at the mention of its name. 'Sir?'

'Can you make porridge, Trugg?' Clara asked.

'Yes miss.' It took the robot less than two seconds to come up with a response. Clara guessed it was downloading something from its memory banks. 'It's simply a case of programming the effluent recyclers to extract the correct ratios of beta-glucan isolates, saturated fats, cholesterol, carbohydrates and—'

'On second thoughts let's forget the porridge,' said the Doctor.

'This is like looking for a needle in a haystack,' complained Laker. 'Only without a needle or a haystack. There's *nothing* out here.'

'There must be something out here for us,' said Cranmer. 'What are your longest-range scanners?'

'Astrolaser and wide-beam spectronic,' Laker said. 'Make no mistake, the *Alexandria*'s got all the latest gear and it's top of the range. But if there's nothing out there to see, it doesn't matter how good your eyes are.'

'But if we could divide the volume of space around us into segments and check each one in turn, matched to the wormhole chart...'

Laker sighed. 'I'm willing to try anything.'

'There will be something out there,' Jem said. She had been resting in the astrogation coach, looking pale and troubled. 'It's just waiting for us, Dan...'

'The "imperfection"?'

Jem looked down. 'I don't know.'

'Are you all right?'

'I'm just a bit tired. But I really want to do this. I really want to know why we've been brought all the way out here.'

'What are you thinking about?' asked Clara quietly.

She was leaning on one of the outer control panels overlooking the rest of the flight deck.

The Doctor stood next to her, glowering. Clara sometimes thought the power in that frown alone could fix the energy supplies of a large city for weeks.

'Everyone here wants something, Clara. And I'm not talking about breakfast.'

'I know. We all want to find a way out of this, for one thing. Get home. Live our lives. Do some marking.'

'No, I don't mean that. I don't mean just *survival*. Survival is boring. It's the base-line requirement for any life. I'm talking about desire.'

'You're talking about the Glamour.'

'Something's brought us all here, Clara. Lured us through that wormhole. Jem knows it. She *sensed* it.'

'The imperfection?'

'Perhaps.'

The Doctor continued to stare at the clone astrogator. She and Laker were poring over scanner readings, searching for something, anything, in the void. Holographic images floated in the air as they cycled through various views and long-distance sensor sweeps.

'Jem *was* very keen to carry on,' Clara noted. 'She insisted, even when Laker wanted to turn back.'

'Yes, she did.'

'She seems very driven. Could that be due to the Glamour?'

The Doctor shrugged. 'That's the trouble with the Glamour, Clara. It's so difficult to tell. Jem's an astrogation clone, remember – genetically modified to feel sub-etheric fluctuations in dark matter. She's bound to be sensitive to whatever brought us through the wormhole.'

'She said she heard voices,' Clara said.

'Hmmm.'

'You're being mysterious. I hate it when you're mysterious.'

'No you don't. You love it. What about the others?'

'Laker wants to retire to look after Jem. So he needs Balfour's money.'

'Hm-mm.'

'Tibby wants to find what happened to the Phaeron.'

'What about Marco?' wondered the Doctor.

Marco Spritt was standing nearby, smirking and keeping a close eye on Tibby as she bent over the screens. 'I think we all know what he wants,' Clara said in disgust.

'The *Carthage*?' said the Doctor.

'Well, I didn't mean that exactly. But you're right. Although I don't think he's really bothered about what happened to the *Carthage*, he just wants to find his mother. Family is a powerful thing; blood thicker than water and all that.'

'You could be right.'

Clara sat back and thought for a moment. 'OK, so everyone wants something. But none of them need to be under the influence of the Glamour for that.'

'But what about Raymond Balfour?'

Balfour was hovering near the flight controls, where Laker and Jem were studying the long range sensor displays. His hands were thrust into the pockets of his dressing gown. Clara watched him carefully.

'He's one of the richest humans in the galaxy,' said the Doctor. 'He can have anything he wants. He can buy anything he wants. We're not talking about fast spaceships or even planets. Balfour can buy entire star systems. He has several different multi-billion credit accounts at the Bank of Karabraxos alone. So what does he want?'

'Adventure?'

'What do you mean?'

'He's bored. Rich beyond the dreams of avarice, maybe, but bored. He's got nothing to do. Nothing to strive for. So: adventure.'

The Doctor considered. 'You can't buy adventure, Clara.'

'Maybe Balfour thinks he can.'   .

'It doesn't matter. We're still in the dark, either way.' The Doctor straightened up suddenly, his eyes widening. 'Oh!'

'What? There's being mysterious and then there's being very annoying. Which one is this going to be?'

'Genius. I am a *genius!*' The Doctor scrambled down to the forward section where Laker and Jem were busy.

'Annoying, then,' said Clara, and followed him down.

'I've had an idea,' said the Doctor.

Laker sat back in his chair, exasperated. 'Well that's good news, because I'm all out of ideas now.'

Cranmer rubbed his face tiredly. 'We've used every kind of long-range multi-probe and come up with nothing apart from the minute quark and gluon field fluctuations you'd expect in a vacuum. There's absolutely nothing out there but empty space.'

'No there isn't,' said the Doctor. 'There's dark matter. Space is full of it, remember.'

'I think I know what the Doctor's idea is,' said Jem.

'What?' Laker asked, looking between them.

The Doctor looked anguished. 'You won't like it.'

'Why not?'

Jem said, 'I can sense fluctuations in dark matter, remember. It's how I see the universe. It's how I can function as an astrogator.'

Laker was instantly wary. 'Firstly, you're not just a function, you're a person. Secondly, there's no way you're getting back into that astrogation couch.' He turned to look at the Doctor. 'Absolutely no way. You saw what happened last time, it nearly killed her.'

'I know, Captain, but this is important...'

'Important enough to risk her life?'

'All our lives are at risk,' the Doctor said.

'That's what you said last time. We had to unhook Jem from the ship mid-flight and it damned near killed her. And you.'

'But the ship won't be in flight,' the Doctor argued. 'We're drifting. She doesn't have to guide us. She only has to tap into the dark matter to see what's around.'

Jem nodded. 'I might be able to find something the scanners couldn't pick up.'

'Dan's right, Doctor,' said Clara. Laker was trying to be reasonable but she had seen the anguish in his eyes. 'We can't ask Jem to risk her life again.'

'I agree,' said Tanya Flexx. 'It's out of the question.'

'The only other option is to carry on drifting aimlessly in the hope that we might stumble across something in the trackless void out there,' argued the Doctor, stabbing a finger at the holoviewer. 'I don't fancy that much. Do you?'

'I have to put Jem's health first.'

'It's too much to ask of her, Doctor.'

'There's no need to *ask* me,' said Jem sharply. She lay back in the astrogation couch. 'And I can speak for myself. I want to do it. Plug me in.'

'You're certain?' the Doctor asked.

'Yes,' said Jem firmly.

'You're both mad and irresponsible,' said Tanya.

'But alive,' replied the Doctor.

Laker glared at him. 'If anything happens to her…' he began, but then he fell silent and concentrated on attaching the various wires from the couch to Jem's head implants. As each clicked home, a display on the couch console flickered into life.

'Will she be OK?' Clara asked the Doctor.

'Yeah, she'll be fine,' he replied quickly.

Clara looked back at Jem, unconvinced. Wires sprouted from the implants all over her head and the astrogation console was humming again.

'I'm in,' Jem whispered, closing her eyes. The displays pulsed and holographic images glowed in the air around her.

'Just take it easy,' Laker said.

Tanya said, 'First sign of trouble and you're out, clear?'

'I'm all right, I'm all right.'

Clara turned to the Doctor. 'She's not all right, is she?'

'Her mind is tuning into etheric superstrings coded into the non-baryonic dark matter of local space,' the Doctor said quietly. 'No human being should be able to do that. But she's been modified and augmented until she's something *other* than human, Clara. Who can tell if she's all right?'

Jem was breathing deeply. With her eyes closed she looked as if she was asleep. No one made a sound as Laker checked and double-checked the astrogation monitors and holograms.

'Nothing… there's nothing…' he whispered. 'She's drawing blanks on all levels.'

The Doctor pressed the edge of one fist against his lip,

concentrating hard. His eyes flicked between Jem and the holograms. His eyebrows formed a deep V as he willed the astrogator to find something… anything… in the depthless void.

Laker toggled through a series of holograms, which mostly looked to Clara like different, darkly coloured smudges hanging in the air. 'Still nothing,' he said.

The Doctor had clenched his fist so tight that his knuckles were bone-white. 'Come on, Jem… come on…' he muttered. 'Find those axion strings… find the nodes… find *something*.'

Jem's breath quickened slightly. Her fingers twitched. The holograms swirled, flickered, changed.

'She's hurrying,' Laker said. 'Cycling through the levels. She must be running out of time.'

'She can take her time,' the Doctor warned. 'There's no hurry…'

'You don't understand,' Laker said. 'She must be in pain. She's trying to get through as much as she can before it gets too much.'

'Stop her now,' Tanya urged. 'If she's in pain, stop her now.'

'Wait until she finds something,' said the Doctor. 'There must be something. She'll find it.'

Clara looked horrified. 'But if she's in pain?'

'No pain, no gain.'

All attention was focused on Jem. The holograms glowed around the couch as she reached out into the void, extending her consciousness well beyond the confines of the *Alexandria*. Everyone watched in silence; Tibby,

Cranmer and Tanya, Marco, Balfour and Mitch all stood with the Doctor and Clara as Laker checked and rechecked the navigation displays.

Jem suddenly opened her mouth and gasped. 'Got it,' she said.

Laker instantly began to power down the couch as the Doctor leapt forward. His long, nimble fingers scuttled around Jem's head, disconnecting the astrogation leads from the implant sockets. The holograms swirled and faded and the couch monitors dimmed.

'Is she OK?' the Doctor asked.

Laker helped Jem to sit up. She looked exhausted. 'I think so.'

'What did you find?' the Doctor asked.

Jem's eyes were open but they weren't focused on anything in front of her. She opened her mouth to speak but said nothing, as if she was struggling for a way to even begin to describe what she had seen. 'Deep in the darkness…' she whispered. Everyone strained to hear. 'Long distant… nothing more than an echo in the emptiness, like a voice calling for me just on the edge of hearing.'

'A voice?' The Doctor leaned closer. 'What did it say?'

'I don't know. It was unlike anything I have ever heard before. I couldn't understand any of the words – if they were words at all.'

'This is worse than useless,' said Marco.

'You shut your mouth,' snapped Laker, turning quickly.

'It's been a complete waste of time and effort,' Marco insisted loudly.

'Marco, be quiet,' said Tibby. 'Let Jem speak.'

'It's all right, it doesn't matter,' Jem said, raising a pale hand. 'I couldn't understand the voices that I heard, but they were calling for me. For all of us.'

Clara felt a chill run through her. She looked at the Doctor, but his face was impassive, stony, his eyes hooded. It was impossible to tell what he was thinking, but Clara suspected it was nothing good.

'It doesn't sound very likely, I must admit,' said Cranmer. 'Voices in space?'

'It's how Jem interprets the gravitational fluctuations in dark matter,' said the Doctor. 'She's trying to describe the indescribable. Is it any wonder her brain searches for a way to understand it? Genetic modification and surgery can only do so much, after all. The good news is that she found anything at all. The even better news is that it means there *is* something out there. Something we can find.' He pointed at Laker. 'Run through the astrogation record, Captain; there'll be coordinate data for the moments when Jem heard the voices. Match them to our current location and see what happens.'

Laker got to work on the sensor array as the Doctor stalked around the flight deck, suddenly bristling with energy. 'We're searching for something invisible, hiding in the darkness… But we have one advantage now: *we know it's there.*'

Clara felt her pulse quickening, as if she was walking through a darkened room, hand out in front of her, groping for a wall, a piece of furniture, anything she could touch. It was at once exciting and terrifying.

'Got it.' Laker turned from the sensor array to face them. His face showed a strange mixture of shock and excitement. 'The Doctor was right. Jem's found something.'

Chapter

7

The planet was clearly visible. At full magnification, the hologram showed a dull grey sphere, turning slowly in the blackness.

'Dark world,' said Luis Cranmer.

'Not quite,' replied Laker. 'You can't see it on screen but there is a sun, with this as the single orbiting planet.'

'What's a dark world?' asked Clara.

'An orphaned planet, adrift in space without a star to orbit,' explained the Doctor. He was studying the holograph image intently. 'But this isn't one of those – look at that faint light, reflecting from the surface. This is an orphaned solar system, a tiny singular world and its sun, lost between the galaxies. Nowhere to call home.'

Cranmer was pulling up more data on the planet from the ship scanners. 'The sun's a non-rotating neutron star, barely detectable. Plenty of thermal radiation, though.'

'A dying star,' the Doctor said. 'Bleeding out into the vacuum.'

'The planet's small – around 7,000 kilometres in diameter but with a 5.5 grams per cubic centimetre density. Gravity will be around Earth normal.'

'How far away are we?' the Doctor asked.

'About 70,000 AU.'

'Just over a light year.'

'Doesn't really matter, though, if we don't have engine power,' said Laker.

There was a grim silence as everyone stared at the hologram. The magnification and resolution were so good the planet felt close enough to touch. There were ridges that were probably mountain ranges and dark, foggy swirls that might be clouds.

'What we need is a miracle,' said Mitch Keller.

'Yeah,' said Hobbo, who had ventured onto the flight deck for the first time to see what was going on. 'Somethin' that makes a joke out of time and space would be good.'

'Mockery was the word I used,' said the Doctor without taking his eyes off the planet. 'But you can forget about my TARDIS. You don't need it. We can get there in the *Alexandria*. All you have to do is run the secondary power elements through the hyperspace field coils and fire the engines up.'

'What?' said Mitch.

The Doctor looked at them as if the answer was obvious. 'Don't tell me you hadn't thought of that?'

'It's stupid,' declared Hobbo. She folded her arms and scowled to show how certain she was. 'Impossible.'

'Trust me,' said the Doctor, 'it'll work.'

Mitch and Hobbo exchanged a look. They were standing in the engine room with the Doctor. He'd come down and scanned the generator units with some kind of portable diagnostic tool he kept in his jacket pocket. Its green light had played over the ion drive for a few seconds and the Doctor seemed happy with the result.

'Your basic problem is a loss of drive power,' he explained. 'The hyperdrive generators will still function if they can be activated. Use the secondary ion drive elements.'

'Can't be done,' Hobbo said. 'Besides, I can't find my ion bonder. It's disappeared from my toolbox.'

'You don't need an ion bonder,' Mitch said. 'You can do it manually. It would be messy, but I think the Doc may have a point, Hobbo.'

She looked at Mitch as if he was mad. '*Messy?* I don't mind messy. But this… well if it worked it would be…it would be…'

'A miracle?'

'Here,' said the Doctor. He tossed the tool over to Hobbo and she caught it. 'Sonic screwdriver. Try setting gamma alpha two pi and then restart the generators.'

Hobbo examined the screwdriver. It was heavy, with some sort of transceiver filament set into steel claws with a copper and ivory handle. She'd never seen anything like it before. She spun it in the air and caught it again. She shrugged. 'Give us an hour,' she said, and headed aft towards the hyperdrive generators.

'Can she do it?' the Doctor asked Mitch.

The old man laughed. 'In her sleep. Most of what I've got up here –' he tapped his head – 'is obsolete. Hobbo's the future.'

'They say old space engineers don't retire…'

'… they just break down.' Mitch shrugged. 'Maybe so. I only came on this trip as a favour to Dan Laker. I was his engineer when he was a young, hotshot pilot in the Space Service.'

'And Hobbo?'

'Found her in the Vandelisco shipyards. She was just a station rat but she knew how to field strip an ion engine by the time she was 10. Self-taught. A natural. The authorities were gonna augment her an' plug her into the service program so I took her with me instead.' Mitch gave a sniff. 'Never had much time for the authorities.'

'Me neither,' said the Doctor.

'I don't like the look of that planet,' Marco said to Tanya Flexx.

They were standing by the main flight deck hologram, close enough to touch it if they could. In fact, Marco had reached out towards the tiny grey world as it revolved slowly in the air. It looked like a ball of coal floating in pool of ink. His fingers met the surface of the image and then passed through, as if there was nothing there.

Tanya shivered. 'It looks so cold and dark.'

'I doubt it will be a very hospitable,' agreed Cranmer. He was checking the data display on a handheld computer. 'I've downloaded the initial long-range scans from the *Alexandria*. The planet is small but dense, which means it will have sufficient gravity and possibly an atmosphere. But the air will most likely be poisonous. I'm getting ammonium hydrosulphide, water ice, methane ice… The surface will also be subjected to a dangerous amount of electron bombardment and radiation from the neutron star.'

'We'd be jumping straight from the frying pan into the fire, then,' said Tanya.

'But the Doctor said we'd come out of the wormhole for a reason,' Tibby argued. 'That planet must be significant. It's the only other thing around here apart from us.'

'*The Doctor said*...' echoed Marco scornfully. 'I don't put as much store in what the Doctor says as you seem to. And I don't think Cranmer does either.'

Cranmer scratched at his beard. 'There is no real evidence to support anything the Doctor has said so far.'

Tibby gave an exasperated sigh. 'But if there is a chance, any chance at all, of finding a clue to what happened to the Phaeron on that planet... then we should at least investigate it. We've come all this way... It would seem pointless to turn back now.'

Marco's lips pressed into a thin line. He wasn't happy. 'Well, if that's what you think, Professor... I'll go along with that. But I still don't trust the Doctor.'

'What do you mean?' Cranmer asked.

'He's keeping something from us. He knows more than he's letting on.'

'You're imagining it,' said Tibby.

'Am I? Then why didn't he tell them how to fix the engines earlier? Come to think of it, how did he know there would be a planet out here?' Marco looked across the flight deck to where the Doctor had just returned from the engine room. He was talking to his pretty young friend.

'They're up to something, I tell you. They've got their own plans – and they're nothing to do with us.'

'Something's up with Jem,' Clara told the Doctor when he returned to the flight deck.

The Doctor went straight to the astrogation couch, where Jem was lying back in her seat, her eyes closed and breathing shallow. Laker was examining the couch instruments with a worried frown while Tanya looked over Jem.

'I think she's slipping into a coma,' said Tanya.

The Doctor quickly examined Jem's head. 'Overload in the primary neural implant.' He sounded angry. 'What is it with you people? Always tinkering and fiddling with what nature gave you. If it's not safety pins through your noses or studs in your tongues it's cranial implants and cerebral hardwiring! Why do this kind of thing to each other?'

'We need to remove the implant,' Laker said. He fished in a drawer on the astrogation console and took out a slim metal box. Inside was a small array of metal rods. It looked to Clara like a cross between a set of surgical instruments and a tool box. He paused for a second and then handed it to Tanya Flexx.

'The augmentation sockets in Jem's skull interface with a superconductor matrix imprinted on the brain,' the Doctor explained to Clara. 'It should be possible to remove a socket without damaging the matrix.'

'Right,' said Clara, feeling none the wiser.

'Listen, Jem,' said Tanya softly. 'We're going to have to take out your primary neural implant, OK?'

She nodded once but her eyes stayed shut. She was clearly in pain.

'I'll be as quick as I can,' Tanya said. She looked at the Doctor and Laker. 'Can you hold her?'

The Doctor placed his hands on either side of Jem's head to keep it still. Laker moved into a better position and held her shoulders. Using a tool from the box Tanya set to work. She appeared to be an expert. Clara estimated that it took barely a minute to unlatch whatever held the implant in place and slowly remove it. It looked like a small metal cylinder which extended a centimetre or so into Jem's skull.

'Thank you,' whispered Jem.

Tanya handed the cylinder to the Doctor and deftly filled the hole with a blank from the tool box. 'No problem,' she said.

'Is there anything I can do?' asked Clara. Watching it was making her feel queasy and she thought it might help if she could get involved somehow.

'Sure.' Tanya handed her the box. 'There's an antiseptic beam and dressing in there.'

Clara checked the box and found the right tools. The antiseptic beam looked like a small penlight and, according to the instructions printed on it, would destroy any germs in the affected area with a three-second blast. She busied herself with this while the Doctor examined the implant Tanya had removed.

'Connection foil is burnt out,' the Doctor said. 'It's useless now.' He threw it away in disgust. 'It was always useless.'

'Jem never asked to be made like this,' said Laker angrily, 'but I've always done the best I can for her. It wasn't me who did the augmentation.'

The Doctor said nothing. Perhaps he didn't know what to say.

Jem opened her eyes and smiled at Laker. 'It's OK. Stop worrying.'

'That's easy for you to say.'

'We're still here. We're still together. That's all that matters.'

'Yeah.' He squeezed her hand and forced out a smile.

'In ancient times, people used to give faulty tech a damn' good whack,' said Mitch. 'Solid state electronics. It often worked.'

Hobbo was crawling into an access hatch on the big, shiny unit that housed the hyperspace generator coils. 'Hurray for the old days.'

'Hey. Don't judge me by my face. These are laughter lines, that's all.'

Mitch was leaning on one of the engine blocks to watch Hobbo work. The engine block was worryingly cold. In truth he was sceptical about the Doctor's idea - but they had to try *something* and it was important to keep Hobbo busy.

A flickering green glow lit up the inside of the hatch and a trilling whine could be heard every time Hobbo used the Doctor's screwdriver. After a few more minutes, Hobbo's voice echoed from deep inside the coil unit: 'This is the coolest thing *ever*.'

'Is that you being positive about somethin'?' Mitch asked. 'Cos if it is, you should give me some warning. I'm too old for shocks.'

'I thought it was astronic radiation that turned your hair white?'

'Watch it, kid.'

Hobbo wriggled back out from the access hatch, her hair more messed up than ever and a big smudge of oil on her face. The screwdriver was clamped between her teeth and she let it drop into her hand so she could speak. 'Are you just gonna sit there and watch?'

'Hey, I'm in charge around here. You do all the dirty jobs and I sit and watch. That's the way it works.'

'Since when?'

'Since forever. When I was your age I was knee-deep in sump fluid, tryin' to stop astronic reactors goin' into thermic collapse every five minutes. I didn't see daylight for three weeks on one ship.'

Hobbo smirked. 'Must've been hard in the olden days.'

'Now you're lookin' all cheerful again. Get back to work.'

She flipped the sonic screwdriver over in her hand and disappeared back into the hyperspace generator. 'At least we've finally got somethin' to do aboard this ship!'

Clara had taken the Doctor to one side. 'Stop being so hard on Laker,' she said quietly. 'He's doing his best for Jem.'

'I think she's suffering more than he is,' said the Doctor, tapping his head meaningfully.

'I seem to recall it was your idea to reconnect her to the ship.' Clara looked at the pilot and Jem as they held hands.

Laker was chewing his lip in consternation. 'Anyway, sometimes it's harder watching someone you love suffer. Will she be all right?'

'She's weak,' the Doctor said, as if he needed to fill the silence that had sprung up between them. 'But Laker keeps her strong. She'll survive.'

A deep whine filled the room and lights flashed on all around the flight deck. Everyone looked at each other in sudden, hopeful surprise. The whine deepened and a faint vibration swelled through the ship.

'Please tell me that's the engines starting up,' said Clara.

More lights came on across the flight consoles. Laker turned in his seat and began operating the controls. 'Power's back in the hyperdrive generators. They did it! Ladies and gentlemen, we're flying again.'

There was a series of claps and small cheers. Raymond Balfour looked as if he was about to cry with relief and Tanya actually hugged Cranmer. Jem was smiling at Laker as he busied himself at the controls. He seemed to be sitting straighter, a look of calm focus on his face as he slipped back into the routine checks and preparations for his trade. The whole flight deck felt suddenly brighter.

The doors opened and Mitch and Hobbo sauntered in to a small round of applause. Hobbo wore a weird half-smile half-frown. Mitch was wiping his hands on a rag.

Balfour crossed the deck to greet them. 'Well done,' he said. 'Absolutely marvellous! I knew you could do it.'

'Well, we're under way, an' that's all that counts now,' Mitch said. 'But it's the Doctor an' Hobbo you should be thanking. It was his idea, an' she did the donkey work.'

'Hey, Doc,' said Hobbo. She threw the sonic screwdriver across the deck and the Doctor snatched it out of the air. 'That tool is freakin' awesome.'

'I prefer "multi-purpose",' replied the Doctor, 'but thanks anyway.'

'Next time you don't get it back.'

'OK, everyone,' announced Laker. 'We're officially a spaceship again. Where to?'

The Doctor pointed to the hologram of the planet. 'I think we all know the answer to that.'

'Maybe we should vote on the matter,' suggested Cranmer. 'If we've got power then we shouldn't waste it.'

'Well that's just the thing,' said Mitch. He tipped his baseball cap back and scratched his forehead. His tone was serious enough to get everyone's attention. 'We've got the ion drive back online so we can move again. But we've had to divert all power to the engines.'

There was a pause while he let the words sink in.

'So is there a problem?' asked Marco.

'*All power*,' repeated Hobbo with heavy emphasis.

'We can move,' Mitch said, 'but everythin' else is gone. There's no power left over. That means the life-support systems are all offline. That means no more air, food or water.'

'We've got enough to last us, surely?' asked Tibby.

Mitch shrugged. 'I'm sorry, miss. Food and drink on this ship is only generated when it's needed. We can't do that now. And as for how long the air will last – I just don't know. We're in a sealed system and there's eleven of us all breathin' the same air.'

'So this is no longer a spaceship at all,' said Cranmer. 'It's a flying coffin.'

Chapter

8

'We either suffocate in here, or land on a planet where the air is toxic,' said Marco Spritt. 'Is that supposed to be a choice?'

The *Alexandria* was en route to the lost planet, travelling at full speed. Laker had estimated that it would take them no more than an hour to get there.

'We have spacesuits,' said Balfour. His voice was shaky, as if he was struggling to take in the enormity of the situation. 'State-of-the-art environmental survival suits. I ordered them especially. The best on the market. They'll keep us alive.'

'Yes, but for how long?' asked Tanya Flexx.

'Each suit has enough air and filters to last seventy-two hours,' said Laker. 'Food and water is the problem.'

'So we have a maximum of three days living in a spacesuit,' said Tanya, throwing her hands up in the air. 'Fantastic.'

'I can't think of anything else,' snapped Balfour.

Clara felt sorry for him. Not even Trugg could help him out of this; and no amount of money could save them

now. But there was something. She and the Doctor had
an ace up their sleeve. She turned to him and gave him a
meaningful look.

Typically, he just raised his eyebrows and said, 'What?'

Clara mouthed the word 'TARDIS'.

The Doctor didn't look happy. He rarely looked happy,
but now there was a particularly strange look in his eyes
beneath the furious brows. The Doctor didn't throw the
doors of the TARDIS open to just anyone, but Clara knew
that in a matter of life and death he wouldn't hesitate. The
TARDIS was the ultimate sanctuary, after all. Plenty of
room and the power to disappear in the blink of an eye. It
could take them all to the dark planet, or back to the space
station, or back to Earth itself. For one giddy moment,
Clara even remembered the pile of marking that awaited
her at home.

But if the Doctor seemed reluctant to mention the
TARDIS, Mitch Keller had no such qualms. He'd already
reached the same conclusion as Clara.

'What about your ship, Doctor?' he asked. 'The blue
box.'

'Are you nuts?' said Hobbo. 'It's nowhere near big
enough. Eleven of us, remember. That thing couldn't hold
more than four or five at a push.'

'And that's not including Trugg,' said Balfour. The robot
gave a mute whirr but said nothing.

All eyes were now on the Doctor. 'Well, I'm sure we
could all squeeze in,' he said with a dismissive flick of his
fingers. 'But that's hardly the point.'

Marco exploded angrily. 'Hardly the point? If you've

got a lifeboat on board then take us to it! I don't care how much of a squeeze it is.'

'I agree with Marco,' said Cranmer. 'Let's get out now if we can.'

'You see?' Marco said triumphantly.

There was a brief clamour as everyone tried to speak at once, but the Doctor's voice rose above all the others. 'Shut up, all of you. Especially you, Marco.'

'Now look here…' Marco began, but the Doctor glared at him and held up one rigid finger for silence. Marco fell quiet.

'Yes, I do have a space-time capsule aboard the *Alexandria*,' said the Doctor. 'It's called the TARDIS, and it is miraculous but there is a good reason why it can't be used now. Tell them, Mr Cranmer.'

Cranmer looked startled as everyone turned to him.

'Come on, man, you've been using your computer to run scans on the planet ever since we found it. Density, atmosphere, radiation, the lot.' The Doctor raised his eyebrows. 'Tell everyone what else you've found.'

'Well,' Cranmer said, peering down at his computer display again. 'It's quite remarkable, actually. I confess that I don't understand it completely. But it appears that there are some extraordinary spatio-temporal phenomena occurring on or around the planet.'

'What's that supposed to mean?' asked Marco.

'There is a layer, or a shell, of chronons and anti-chronons surrounding the planet in a highly agitated state, throwing off a storm of loose tachyons and Hawking radiation.'

'I don't understand,' said Tibby. 'Can't you explain it a little better?'

'The readings are unusual and difficult to interpret,' Cranmer said, 'but there appear to be overlapping spheres of discrete time surrounding the planet.'

'Oh, that makes it a lot clearer,' said Marco with heavy sarcasm.

'He means it's not just any old toxic planet lost in deep space,' said the Doctor. 'I couldn't materialise my TARDIS there even if I wanted to. The temporal interference would act as an impenetrable barrier to a time machine.'

He paused, making sure that he had everyone's complete attention.

'There's only one way onto that planet – and that's in the *Alexandria*.'

'But why do we have to go there at all?' asked Cranmer.

'It's what we came for, isn't it?' said Tibby crossly.

'It's certain death!' Cranmer said. 'Seventy-two hours' air, remember.'

'You can do a lot in seventy-two hours,' said Tibby.

The Doctor's fingers clicked loudly and he pointed at Tibby. 'Correct.'

No one looked as if this was the most reassuring thing they'd heard all day, but the Doctor seemed not to notice, because at that moment the *Alexandria* rocked slightly and everyone had to reach out for something to hold.

'We've been caught in some kind of gravitational field,' said Laker. His hands were busy at the flight controls, adjusting to the sudden turbulence.

'It's the charged chronon layer,' said Cranmer, tapping

his computer. 'It's creating some kind of gravity vortex, pulling us in…'

The planet suspended in the holoviewer looked suddenly very close. Clouds swirled across the surface, tracing the paths of continental storms flickering with electrical charge.

'What we're seeing now are real time pictures at full scale,' said Laker, making another adjustment to the controls. 'Whatever's happening on that planet, we're seeing it now.'

The planet was growing larger by the second as the *Alexandria* moved into orbit, rocking from side to side as it flew through the chronon fields. A web of blue and purple light, pulsing like the arterial veins, flickered across the surface and drew great clouds of darkness into the atmosphere.

'Best get your spacesuits on,' announced Laker. 'This could get rough.'

For a moment nobody moved. It was almost as if no one could quite believe it had actually come to this. Suddenly the prospect of wearing a spacesuit was very uninviting, but a further shudder through the *Alexandria* focused minds very quickly.

'The suits are all here,' said Balfour, touching a wall control. A series of panels slid noiselessly aside to reveal plastic packs in recessed units. Trugg moved forward and began to hand out the packs to everyone on the flight deck.

'The spacesuits are made from the latest steelex conform mesh with chain-molecule superglass helmets and fully compressed oxygen rods,' said Trugg.

'We don't need the sales pitch now,' said Balfour. 'Just give them out.'

Clara took one of the packs from Trugg and found it to be much lighter than she expected. Future materials, she guessed; presumably very durable but without much weight. She unsealed the pack and removed a metallic blue one-piece similar to a wetsuit. The material was soft and extremely flexible; nothing like the bulky suit she had once worn on the Moon.

'Put it on over your clothes,' advised the Doctor, who was already pushing his legs into the suit from his own pack. 'The material will expand to whatever size is needed. It should be able to manage, even with you.'

'Thanks,' Clara said drily. She pulled on the spacesuit and discovered that it automatically adjusted itself and sealed without her having to do anything at all.

The Doctor looked even skinnier than normal in his spacesuit. He was already pulling on slim white boots and a pair of matching gloves. Clara did the same, and found that these too sealed themselves to the rest of the suit. It was surprisingly comfortable and warm.

'Helmets,' said Balfour as Trugg distributed a number of transparent globes fitted to flexible collars. To Clara they looked rather fragile, and she hesitated to put it on.

'Don't worry,' said the Doctor, rapping a knuckle against his own space helmet. 'It's unbreakable – a kind of chain-molecule polymer with a polarising light filter. You could chuck a house brick at it and it won't even scratch.'

'The name tag will activate according to your vital

signs,' Balfour said. 'Doctor, Miss Oswald, you may have to put yours in manually.'

There was a digital display embedded in the glass. After a moment or two Clara worked out how to use it and typed CLARA. 'Where are the oxygen tanks? What do we breathe?'

The Doctor indicated a small device attached to the back of the helmet. 'Compact life-support unit with solid oxygen rods. That's enough air for three days; two if you spend it running up a hill.'

'Let's hope there are no hills, then,' Clara said, pulling the helmet on. It clicked into place on the collar of her suit and she heard the pneumatic hiss of the seal engaging. For a moment everything seemed muffled until the air system activated and some kind of transceiver allowed sound in and out of the globe.

'You've got atmospheric audio pick-up now,' Balfour advised them. 'In vacuum conditions you'll need to switch to radio comms. Each suit has its own transponder. The controls are on your sleeves; you can adjust the environmental settings as well if you want, although the suits are all thermostatic.'

'Where do we sit?' asked Tibby. She was helping Luis Cranmer into his suit.

'There's a bank of emergency seating situated behind the captain's chair,' Balfour said. 'It's a standard safety feature on all *Heracles*-class starships, but these have been updated with—'

'Yes, yes,' said Marco. 'Just get on with it!'

Trugg operated a control and two rows of chairs rose

smoothly out of the deck behind the captain's chair and the astrogation couch. The seats were tilted back at an angle and had safety bars fitted. They reminded Clara uncomfortably of the seats in a theme park rollercoaster.

The ship was shaking quite a lot now and it was getting difficult to stand upright. Clara was surprised to see that the holographic view of the planet had flattened out into nothing more than a vast, curved horizon and black sky. They had already reached the upper atmosphere and the *Alexandria* was starting to feel it.

'All set?' Laker called back. 'Better sit down and strap in.'

'It's been a while since I had to strap in for landing,' said Mitch.

'I bet you had to do it all the time in the old days,' said Hobbo. 'You and Neil Armstrong.'

'Cute,' Mitch replied. 'Real cute.'

Marco had already taken his place in the row behind Laker and Jem and, as there was nowhere else to go, Clara and the Doctor sat with him. Cranmer eased himself carefully into the seat next to Clara. He didn't look happy; his face was sweating profusely inside his helmet. Clara tried to think of something wittily reassuring to say but couldn't. She settled for giving him a brief smile, which she suspected looked more like a worried grimace.

'I hope this is over quickly,' he said, closing his eyes.

'Right,' said Laker, raising his voice over the noise of the turbulence. 'I'm switching to radio. Channel 1 on your suits.'

They all inspected the controls on their forearms and selected the right channel. Instantly Laker's voice sounded inside their helmets, as clear as if he was standing right next to them.

'I'm taking us in as best I can but it's not going to be pretty. Autopilot can only do so much, so the rest is down to me. If we crash, it's the computer's fault. If we make it, then it's mine.'

'You'll be great,' said Jem. 'Go for it.'

The *Alexandria* was skirting the planetary atmosphere, bumping and jolting every time the underside of the ship touched the edge. A screaming sound began to build up as the ship nosed deeper into the air. They were still some way above the cloud layer, but already they seemed to be coming in at a very steep angle.

Clara reached out and grabbed the Doctor's hand. It was purely instinctive. 'Not done this before,' she said. 'One to cross off the bucket list.'

'There's nothing to worry about,' the Doctor said.

'Are you sure?' asked Luis Cranmer nervously.

Clara suddenly remembered they were talking on an open channel, and everyone could hear the conversation.

'Actually, there's quite a lot to be worried about,' said the Doctor. 'Gravity for one thing, of course. That's the main problem. Get that one wrong and *splat*! The ride's over.'

Cranmer swallowed audibly and turned back to face the hologram of the planet. The clouds were rushing up to meet them, thin streams of vapour whipping past the ship as it dived towards the surface.

'Gravity will pull us down towards the surface all right – but luckily for us there's an atmosphere, which will cause friction if we keep the angle of re-entry just right.

That'll help to slow us down.'

'Won't we burn up or something?' asked Cranmer.

'Well that's the problem with friction. The temperature will shoot right up and if it gets too hot the ship will ignite and we'll all be incinerated in a gigantic fireball.'

Cranmer groaned and closed his eyes. 'I think I'm going to puke.'

'Don't,' warned the Doctor. 'Spacesuit. Not a good idea.'

'It hardly matters if I'm going to be burnt alive!'

'Ah, but the blunt shape of the *Alexandria* will create an ablative shockwave as it passes through the atmosphere,' explained the Doctor. 'That shockwave will keep the worst of the heat away. Plus the hull is made from a special material which will absorb a lot of the heat. So no worries there.'

'You mean we're going to be OK?'

'Yes,' said the Doctor. 'We're going to be OK.'

Clara felt something move beneath her hand and looked down. The Doctor had crossed his fingers.

Chapter

9

The *Alexandria* skimmed the edge of the atmosphere, throwing off plumes of superheated plasma before plunging towards the planet's surface.

The ship immediately began to buckle under the intense changes in atmospheric pressure. Exterior panels bent and twisted and peeled away from the hull, disappearing in a stream of molten alloys. Insulation layers bubbled and trailed lines of black smoke. The *Alexandria* drew a long, dark scar across the steel-coloured sky and disappeared into a gigantic storm cloud.

Laker could barely see the holoviewer. The ship was vibrating so badly it was impossible to focus. He glimpsed layers of cloud rushing towards him, and flashes of lightning which were so bright they left him momentarily blinded. He concentrated on keeping the vessel under control, his hands white and painful with cramp. It took all of his strength to keep the ship level. Toxic clouds whipped past the ship in long, grey streamers. Alarms flashed on the flight controls as the cocktail of acids ate into the hull. Laker ignored them. There was nothing he could do about the acid except hope it didn't touch anything vital. Finally he began to feel the *Alexandria* bouncing against the weak thermals rising from the planetary surface and he activated the aerofoils. The ship was shaking so much it was impossible to tell if the wings were deploying properly. He fought to keep the nose down, aware that with the increased surface area provided by the wings there was a danger the ship could just flip over on its back and die in the air. Sure enough the ship began to roll heavily to starboard and there was a loud scream of rending metal. The *Alexandria* tipped over and Laker gritted his teeth and hauled on the controls. The horizon tilted in the holoviewer, and he saw a blur of land flash past the ship, over his head as it turned completely, and then slide around to the other side as he tried to bring it level.

The *Alexandria* broke out of the heavy cloud layer, and Laker realised to his dismay that the ground was much closer than he'd thought. The ship was diving towards a rocky landscape and warning alarms fired off around the flight deck as the altitude, pitch, roll and yaw sensors all went into the red. He'd lost control. There had been too much damage from the heat of re-entry and the acid clouds.

There was nothing Laker could do now. His hands felt numb on the controls and his mind was blank. He could only watch as the surface of the planet approached in a terrifying blur.

The scream of the *Alexandria*'s dive merged with the screams on the flight deck as the ship hit the ground. Laker did his best to pull the craft up enough to take the hit and slide, but even so the noise was deafening, and Clara felt herself thrown forward so hard she thought the seatbelt would break every rib she had. The breath rushed out of her lungs in one convulsive blast and for a moment she lost all consciousness.

The noise woke her. It sounded like her alarm clock and briefly she thought it was morning and time to get up. But then the alarm sound mingled with the noise of tearing metal and she opened her eyes to see a huge section of the flight deck roof sagging towards her. Pieces of blackened plastic and debris from exploded control consoles littered every surface. Black smoke curled around figures in spacesuits fumbling their way out of the seats. Flames flickered in dark recesses, licking out hungrily for something more substantial to devour. The alarm noise, Clara slowly realised, was an alert sounding in her suit helmet. Entoptic displays glowed on the transparent visor, warning her of toxic vapour. She began to scrabble at the buckle on her seatbelt but she couldn't get a proper grip with her gloves. Cranmer sat rigidly beside her, probably frozen with terror.

Someone was talking to her. A spacesuited figure loomed out of the smoke. On the helmet was the word DOCTOR. 'Come on, Clara, we have to get out of here quickly.'

'Is the ship going to blow up?' she asked. Wasn't that what happened when things crashed?

'I don't think so, but we have to get out. It's not stable. The hull superstructure could collapse at any moment.'

Clara fumbled at her seatbelt again but the Doctor knocked her hands away and unfastened it himself, hauling her out of the seat. She was shaky, barely able to feel her legs. She flinched when another sudden squeal of tortured metal accompanied the roof as it buckled under its own weight. Electronics, exposed in the gaping wounds between the metal panels, bled gouts of bright sparks and then torrents of flame.

The others were milling around, helping each other towards the exit. She saw Tanya Flexx helping Balfour climb over some wreckage towards a half-collapsed doorway. The wreckage was the remains of Trugg. The robot had been crushed beneath falling debris; none of his lights were flashing any more.

'Trugg's gone,' Clara said sadly.

'I'm afraid so,' said the Doctor. 'Come on, we have to hurry.'

'What about Cranmer?' she asked, turning to the seat next to her.

'He won't be coming with us either.'

It took a moment for Clara to comprehend what she saw. A long metal roof stanchion had broken off during the impact and landed on Cranmer. His space helmet had been completely smashed. Clara looked away instantly. A numb sense of shock and repulsion flooded through her. It wasn't even the physical damage; it was more the unbelievable sensation that Cranmer, the person, the personality, was gone. Gone forever. Extinguished in a second. Half a metre to the left and the stanchion could have gone through her instead. Clara didn't feel any sense of relief or guilt, just a strange, fluttering, shaky feeling right in the centre of her body.

She let the Doctor lead her away from the seats, numb and cold. He took her to the exit, stepping over bits of machinery and wreckage that Clara didn't even recognise. 'Go with Mitch and Hobbo. Help the others, Clara, they need organising.'

She responded as he knew she would, following Mitch and Hobbo as they climbed over Trugg's crushed remains and led the way out of the wreck. Some of the interior passageways had collapsed and they had to crawl through narrow gaps between the jagged edges of torn bulkhead.

'Watch your suits,' Mitch advised.

Clara stuck with Hobbo and together they inched their way to the main exit. Smoke filled the passageways, and sometimes they had to grope their way along. Any moment, Clara feared, she would catch her glove on a sharp piece of metal and tear it open. Liquid dripped through gaps in the roof, and as it ran down the walls and formed cloudy pools on the floor, Clara saw thin wisps of smoke rising from the puddles. Acid rain, of course.

After what seemed an age they climbed down the twisted remains of the landing ramp and out onto the surface of an alien world. Clara didn't feel in the mood to appreciate it. The air was foggy with smoke, the ground hard and rocky and grey as ashes. It reminded her of the Moon, only here there was a sky – greenish grey and streaked with low, churning clouds. Rain speckled her suit and visor and left faint patches where the acid tried to burn through.

Tibby Vent stood with Tanya and Marco a few metres

away. Clara clambered up the flinty slope towards them with Mitch and Hobbo. Loose earth had been thrown up by the impact, and Raymond Balfour sat at the top, looking at his beloved *Alexandria*. With a terrible groaning of strained metal, the whole thing lurched forwards.

'It's hanging over a precipice,' said Balfour. There were tears on his face, and his voice, full of emotion, sounded loud inside Clara's helmet. Everyone looked towards the front of the *Alexandria* and saw that he was right – the bows were suspended in the air, with the rest of the craft seemingly embedded in the edge of a cliff. The flight deck extended out over the edge, like a swan peering into the abyss.

'It must be a thousand metres down, or maybe more,' Tanya Flexx said dully. 'We've landed right on the edge of some kind of escarpment.'

The *Alexandria* lurched again, sliding further over the edge. It wasn't embedded in the cliff; it was only resting there. Precariously. Even as they watched in mute disbelief the entire spacecraft tilted again, slid further over the edge and then gradually stopped. Crumbling rock and earth, dislodged by the movement, tumbled away over the cliff edge. The gap left caused the ship to slide even further, until it began to tip right up, teetering like an arrow balanced on the edge of a table. Inevitably it was going to go all the way over.

'Where's the Doctor?' Clara asked.

'He stayed on board to help Laker,' said Hobbo. 'They're trying to get Jem out.'

*

Inside the spaceship, the Doctor and Laker examined the astrogation couch. It was partially crushed under the weight of the collapsed hologram display unit and the compression of the roof. Smoke billowed from cracks in the floor, making it impossible to see anything clearly for more than a few seconds.

'Please hurry,' said Jem. They could both hear her over the helmet communicators. The Doctor was on all fours, his visor pressed up against the worst of the damage, flapping his hand to try and waft away the worst of the smoke.

'We're trying,' said Laker. 'But something's got you caught tight.'

'I can't move.'

'Try not to panic. We need to free whatever's causing the problem, but without tearing your suit. The Doctor's checking it out now.'

'We don't have time,' Jem said.

'I'm not leaving without you,' Laker told her. He grabbed the Doctor's arm. 'Any luck?'

'The bulkhead support has twisted the couch frame out of shape,' the Doctor said. 'The seat restraints are stuck fast.'

'Would a knife cut through them?'

'It might, if we had one,' the Doctor said. 'Fortunately I have something a little better than that.' He held up his sonic screwdriver, which he had put in one of the utility pockets on the leg of his spacesuit.

'We can get her out?'

'I wouldn't still be here if we couldn't.' The Doctor

aimed the screwdriver at the seat restraints and it whirred busily. He cycled up through a variety of settings. 'It's just a case of finding the right frequency…'

The ship shook and lurched forward and Jem let out a gasp. 'Hurry up, please!'

'Shh,' said the Doctor. 'Concentrating. I'm trying to get the right frequency to dissolve titanium poly-tritillium. It's hard enough to say, let alone dissolve, so I suggest you keep quiet and let me work it out.'

The Doctor worked feverishly for several seconds and the screwdriver made a series of bleeps, buzzes and whistles as he experimented with the settings.

'We don't have much time, Doctor,' Laker said as the ship's superstructure groaned and flexed.

'Give me an E-sharp,' said the Doctor.

'What?'

'Sing! I need a note for the screwdriver. Give me an E-sharp! Didn't they teach you anything useful at space pilot school?'

'Not how to sing, no!'

'They didn't even have a choir?'

'No!'

'I'll just have to do it myself then, as usual,' the Doctor muttered. He let out a strange, discordant sound. 'I once auditioned for an Ogron choir. Didn't get in. Apparently there was no vacancy for a light treble! I told them they didn't have any light trebles *at all*. "Exactly," they said. But that's Ogrons for you: obsessed with *Les Mis*. No time at all for *Rigoletto*.'

The sonic screwdriver let out a shrill whistle and

suddenly the straps were free. Jem sprang out of the couch into Laker's arms. He groaned loudly. 'I think I've broken my arm,' he told her.

'Let's do all the mushy stuff later,' advised the Doctor as the ceiling dropped another half meter with a loud, rending clang. 'Before we all become mushy stuff.'

They scrambled through the ship, the Doctor leading the way with Jem and Laker helping each other. Jem was weak, barely able to walk, and, although Laker wanted to carry her, it was impossible with a broken arm. They wriggled through the collapsed sections but the ship kept lurching violently, forcing them to stop and wait before pushing on. By the time they reached the exit, they had to climb up the slope of the floor on their stomachs. When they reached the outside, the exit ramp was suspended three or four metres off the ground. With every grinding second, the ship tilted further forward and the ramp rose higher. On the ground outside, the others were all waiting, calling for them to hurry.

'We're going to have to jump,' the Doctor told Laker.

'You go first,' said Laker. 'You can help catch Jem.'

There was no time to discuss it. The Doctor swung his legs over the edge of the ramp, turned, eased himself part of the way down and then hung by his arms for a moment before letting go. He hit the ground and rolled like an experienced skydiver.

Clara ran down the slope towards him and helped him up. 'Thank God you're out,' she gasped. 'The ship's on the edge of a cliff and it's about to go over.'

The *Alexandria* lurched forward again, the rear end rising

off the ground in a cloud of dust and crumbling rock. The landing ramp rose higher until it was five or six metres off the ground. Laker and Jem's faces peered down from the lip of the ramp.

'Jump!' cried the Doctor. 'Now, before it's too late!'

Jem's face was pale as milk inside her space helmet. 'It's too far!'

'Do it now!'

Laker said, 'You've got to go. Jump! They'll catch you.'

'We go together,' Jem said.

'No, you've got to go first,' Laker implored. 'They can't catch us both together. Only one at a time. Now go. Please. I'll follow you straight away.'

'Jump now or you'll die,' yelled the Doctor. Balfour, Tanya Flexx, Mitch and Hobbo had all gathered beneath the ramp, ready to catch whoever jumped next.

Jem eased forward. Laker appeared behind her and grasped her shoulders. 'Catch her!' he shouted, pushing her off the edge of the ramp as it began to rise again.

Jem screamed for a moment as she fell and then she was caught by the Doctor, Mitch and Clara in tangle of arms and legs and space helmets clacking together. They all tumbled to the ground as the *Alexandria* reared up like a harpooned whale surfacing from the ocean. Dust billowed from beneath the vessel as it slid inexorably forwards and down, diving slowly and purposefully over the edge of the cliff, taking Dan Laker with it.

Chapter

10

A cold wind blew against the cliff and carried with it the last echoes of the *Alexandria*'s demise. The air was heavy, dragging a grey, corrosive mist like a curtain over the crash site.

Clara had watched the *Alexandria* break apart as it fell, bouncing and jolting down the face of the cliff, shedding engines, bulkheads, all kinds of machinery until there was nothing more than a ball of unrecognisable scrap. There could be no doubt that Laker was dead, and it felt like a more desperate loss than Cranmer, whose demise had been instant and unseen. Clara had looked into Dan Laker's eyes as the *Alexandria* slipped over the edge of the cliff and they had both known that he was going to die.

Clara turned away, tears running down her face. She couldn't wipe them away with a space helmet on. They just had to flow.

Jem was sitting on the ground while Tibby and Mitch tried to offer comfort. Clara could see the tears glistening on Tibby's face too, and could see her lips moving as she spoke. It was impossible to know what she was saying.

They'd switched to a private channel. Probably Tibby didn't even know herself.

Jem looked hollowed out. Her eyes were dark. Clara knew that feeling, knew it only too well and she did not offer any words of comfort or condolence because she knew it was pointless. In those first, dark, unknowable moments after losing someone you love, words are just white noise. Life just became something that everyone else got on with. But not you. Not for a long time.

Balfour was standing to one side, alone. The ability to buy anything in the universe had become irrelevant; meaningless. He looked lost without the familiar shape of Trugg looming over him. No wonder Balfour looked so bereft. He hadn't just lost his ship, he'd lost a companion. The robot had seemed like a real person to Clara, and so perhaps it had been, in a way. Cranmer, Laker and Trugg. Gone just like that.

Eventually, Clara found herself back at the cliff edge, which extended in a meandering, jagged line that disappeared into the murky distance. The land stretched away far below, as rugged and unforgiving as could be, shrouded with low, miasmic clouds of acid. The planet seemed to exist in a perpetual dusk, with a lowering sky thick with distant, dark storms. A tiny movement in the air caught Clara's eye and she realised with a start that there were things flying in the lower clouds, some kind of tough, avian creatures impervious to the acid. Clara tried to remind herself that, whatever the circumstances, seeing all this was still a great privilege.

Clara looked for the Doctor. He was around somewhere,

busy doing his Time Lord thing, while the humans tried to come to terms with death. She spotted his lanky, spacesuited figure clambering up from the very edge of the cliff, hand over hand on the rocks, his grey hair standing up inside his helmet, either from static electricity or excitement. Clara took a deep breath and braced herself.

'We have to get down there,' said the Doctor, pointing back towards the cliff edge. 'We have to find the *Alexandria*.'

Before Clara could respond, Marco said, 'What's the point? It's scrap metal now. It's no use to anyone!'

'He's right,' said Tanya Flexx miserably. 'The *Alexandria* is lost. Luis and Captain Laker too.'

'With no ship to fly, we don't need a pilot anyway,' said Marco.

Mitch stepped forward angrily, bunching his fists. 'Why you lousy creep! I oughta…'

The engineer launched himself at Marco, crashing his shoulder into the younger man's chest and sending him staggering backwards. Tibby cried out as Marco fell and, when Mitch went to stamp on him, Balfour and Hobbo both grabbed the old man by his arms and pulled him back.

'You could have killed me, you idiot!' Marco said, his voice shrill with fear and humiliation as he got to his feet.

Mitch's face was flushed with anger. 'Dan Laker was my pal, you little rat,' he snarled. 'If I had my way now, I'd kick you right off that cliff.'

'Just cool it, Mitch,' insisted Hobbo. 'He's not worth it.'

For a moment the two men stood facing each other, breathing heavily, and all that could be heard was Jem's weeping.

The Doctor gave a disgusted sigh. 'That's right, humans. What do you do in a bad situation? Turn on each other. Of course you do.'

Marco glared at him. 'I was only stating the truth.'

'The truth?' The Doctor glared furiously at him. 'The truth is that we're stranded on a planet orbiting a dead star countless light years from anywhere. The only chance we have is down there at the bottom of that cliff and we have less than seventy-two hours to get there, but you want to waste time squabbling like infants!'

'The only chance we have?' Marco scoffed. 'Get real. Don't you understand? The ship's a write-off.'

'My TARDIS was in the hold, remember. It'll still be there.'

'Don't be ridiculous.'

Clara hated to admit it but she too found it difficult to believe anything could have survived, even the TARDIS. Perhaps it was just the grimness of their surroundings, or the loss of life, but she felt as hopeless as she could ever remember.

Mitch was equally sceptical. 'Doc, *nothin'* will have survived that fall.'

'The TARDIS is tougher than it looks,' said the Doctor.

'It would have to be indestructible,' said Hobbo.

'It exists conterminously in five relative dimensions – of course it's indestructible.'

'But how are we going to get down there?' asked Tibby Vent. 'It must be a thousand feet of sheer rock. It's impossible.'

The Doctor said, 'It was impossible for Dan Laker to

land the *Alexandria* the way he did. If it wasn't for his skill and determination, we would be nothing more than a stain on the surface of this planet. What *he* did was frankly impossible and we all owe him our lives, every one of us.'

'Thank you,' said Jem quietly. Everyone else stayed silent.

'Do you think Laker would have wanted us all to give up now? Just because something looks impossible?' the Doctor added.

'But seriously: how are we going to get down there?' asked Marco. 'Climb?'

'Unless you can sprout wings and fly, then yes,' said the Doctor. 'We climb.'

Marco scowled. 'I can't climb down there!'

'That's fine,' said Mitch sourly. 'You stay up here and use up your air supply doing nothing. The rest of us are gonna try an' survive.'

Balfour turned to Marco. 'What choice do we have, Marco? Really?'

Clara said, 'We stick together. We help each other. If anyone needs help then that's fine. Chances are we'll all need help at some point. If we all work together, we can do it. All right?'

Hobbo nodded. 'Yeah, come on. We can do this.'

'I'm not going to argue,' sighed Tanya. 'But let's get on with it before I change my mind.'

Hobbo checked the oxygen supply indicator on the wrist of her spacesuit. 'I'm on seventy hours. That should be more than enough.'

Everyone checked their oxygen level and the condition

of their suits. No one argued. No one discussed anything. Each member of the group looked within themselves for the strength and resolve they personally required. Some found it. Others pretended they had.

Eventually Balfour led the way to the cliff edge, saying that he would go first. The others followed without question, forming an orderly queue. Mitch and Hobbo followed Balfour with Jem, then came Tibby Vent and Tanya Flexx, and finally Marco Spritt. The Doctor and Clara waited until last.

Clara turned to the Doctor and gave him a sad smile. 'Satisfied? We humans can do more than fight, sometimes.'

Doctor nodded, watching each of them traversing the edge of the cliff before starting the long climb down. 'Yes, Clara. Sometimes you can.'

They began the descent slowly. It was a dizzying drop and every handhold and footstep had to be checked and tested in turn. But the cliff was made from a series of horizontal steps which afforded narrow ledges and outcrops every few metres, meaning that they could stop and rest before continuing with the next part of the climb.

'You can see the clear geological strata in the rock,' said the Doctor.

He was right, of course, but Clara couldn't bring herself to be interested. For one thing, she was too busy concentrating on not falling off the cliff to her death. For another, she was still thinking about Cranmer and Laker and Trugg. She couldn't just close off things like that in her mind any more. She knew the Doctor could. She wondered if that was a result of long practice, or just the natural indifference of a Time Lord.

'There are rock types here analogous with sandstone on Earth, Clara,' continued the Doctor, tracing the fingers of one gloved hand along a rough, salmon-coloured horizontal edge in the cliff before him. There was a noticeable change in the hue and texture above and below it. 'Clay, carbonate substrata, shale… the ancient geological history of this world is right here in front of us.'

'I'm a bit more worried about the immediate future, to be honest,' Clara told him. She climbed down the last section of steep slope onto the ledge where the Doctor stood facing the rock.

'It's not as far as you think to the bottom of the cliff,' said the Doctor. The lights inside his suit collar cast a glow on his old, craggy features and made a fuzzy halo of his hair. 'And besides, we've got gravity on our side.'

'That's good, is it?' asked Clara, eyeing the stomach-churning drop.

'Better than having to climb *up* the cliff.'

They climbed down a little further until they caught up with the others. They were getting their breath back, standing together on a generous granite ledge. Balfour was breathing heavily. 'I'm not used to this kind of exertion,' he panted, leaning against the rock face.

'I don't think any of us are,' agreed Tibby.

For a second they all stood in silence, savouring the rest, and let their gaze drift over murky, lifeless vista before them. Mist wreathed the ground hundreds of metres below, but in the distance there were dark, jagged mountain ranges scratching at the cloud base.

'Do you think we're the first humans to visit this world?' asked Tibby.

'We must be,' said Balfour.

'I can't help wondering if the *Carthage* made it here,' said Marco. He looked out across the deep valley below, the endless bare rock and distant, sharp-peaked mountains. 'Although a part of me hopes they didn't. What a disgusting, poisonous world this is.'

'Is that what you see?' asked the Doctor. 'Look again. All of you. What *do* you see? A planet bathed in a lethal cocktail of X-rays and charged particles? Yes. Sunlight from a dying star so faint in visible light that it can barely cast a shadow? Yes. Land masses scoured by acid rain and storms? Absolutely. And yet it's *beautiful*: mountains and valleys, clouds and rain… and over there, look! Birds flying – life! Life doing what life always does: surviving and evolving, and learning to survive better and evolve better every day, no matter what the environment throws at it. That's what we're doing now – exactly the same thing as those birds: surviving. Living! Isn't it a fine thing?'

No one disagreed. They waited another few minutes and then, to everyone's surprise, Marco Spritt led the way forward, with Tibby and Balfour following. Clara came behind them with Mitch and Hobbo.

Jem walked towards the edge of the path in what looked like some kind of trance. The Doctor touched her gently on the arm, and she stopped and looked at him. Her expression remained blank.

'He wanted you to live, you know,' said the Doctor. 'That's why he pushed you out of the ship like that.'

'I know,' she replied. Her voice was dull and flat, almost as if she was uninterested.

'So *live*,' the Doctor told her. 'Take care, look after yourself and treasure your life – because that's what he wanted. And so should you. If you can't yet do it for yourself, then do it for him.'

Jem paused, looked at him. 'What do you know about losing someone you love?'

'Enough. All I'm saying is – don't give up.'

'Why not?'

'Because Dan wouldn't want you to.'

'Dan isn't here any more.'

'*I* don't want you to. Nobody does. And we are all still here – and so are you.'

'And that matters, does it?' Jem turned after she said that, not giving the Doctor time to respond, and climbed down after the others. Her limbs moved with all the unthinking automation of a machine.

The Doctor sighed and followed her.

The birds had started to fly closer. Occasionally one would swoop down, emitting ultrasonic squeals that the spacesuit audio systems could just about detect, and then wheel away. At first they assumed the birds had taken an interest in the climbing party as they inched their way down the cliff, but then it became apparent that they were attracted by something else. Some kind of lichen was growing in the deeper crevices of the rock face – spongy, mustard-coloured lumps the size of cauliflowers – and when these were disturbed in the continuous search for hand and footholds, large, pale lice would creep out of the darker recesses. The birds, as they grew bolder, would fly down, skirt across the face of the cliff and expertly peck at the lice as they passed.

The birds were not birds. Closer views showed them to be some kind of cross between bats and dragonflies. They didn't seem to be a danger to the climbers, but some of them had fibrous wingspans of nearly a metre and more than once they clipped the helmet or legs of someone as they hung against the cliff face.

Marco lashed out at one persistent fly, trying to smash it away with his fist. He failed, but overbalanced, and started to topple away from the narrow path. Just as Marco began to fall, Balfour lunged forward and caught hold of his arm.

For a second they were frozen. Marco, with a look of panic and terror on his face. Balfour, teeth gritted, straining to keep him from plunging to his death. They looked into each other's eyes and understood exactly what had happened. Marco owed Balfour his life at that moment; but there was no gratitude, or relief, only deep resentment.

Without speaking a word to each other, they regained their positions on the cliff and continued the descent.

After a few minutes Clara opened a radio channel to the whole party. 'Did anyone feel that?'

'Feel what?' asked Tanya.

'I thought I felt something move,' Clara said. 'The rock, I mean.'

'Some sort of tremor,' said the Doctor. He was twenty

metres above them, following Jem. 'I felt it too.'

Almost as soon as he finished speaking, there was another tremor. They all felt it this time. The whole rock face shook and loose shale clattered down the cliff.

'What's happening?' Tibby's voice sounded shakily in their helmets.

'I dread to think,' said the Doctor. 'The geology suggests extensive seismic activity in the past, but—'

His words were drowned out by another, longer tremor that they all felt strongly; it was as if the whole cliff was flinching, trying to shake them off.

'Earthquake?' said Clara, couching as low as she could to the narrow ledge she had found. The others were doing the same, or pressing themselves into the rock wall. Rocks and pebbles cascaded past them, some bouncing off their helmets. Clara tried to recall what the Doctor had said about the transparent globes. Something about withstanding a brick thrown at them?

'We can't go back up,' Mitch said. 'We'll just have to carry on.'

'Maybe we should pick up the pace a bit,' suggested Hobbo, but it was clear from the look on Mitch's face that this wasn't really an option. Climbing down the cliff was a slow and difficult process for all of them. Mitch was already struggling. Hurrying was only going to cause accidents.

Nevertheless, by mutual agreement, they continued with the descent, but it wasn't long before a much larger quake hit. A massive shudder ran through several hundred thousand tons of granite and Clara felt her boots slip off the rocks. Her fingers scrabbled for a grip but it was useless. The Doctor went to grab her, but his hand missed hers and she fell. There wasn't even time to scream before she realised that the Doctor, too, had lost his grip and was falling. They all were. No one could hold onto the rock now; it was splitting away from the cliff in great, angular chunks.

And in the space of a few moments, they were all falling. Then Clara found the time to scream.

Chapter

11

Clara woke up feeling warm and comfortable and, just for a second, she thought she was back in her bed, in her flat, waking up for another day at work. But then she realised she was staring up at the sky, not the ceiling; it was iron-grey, like the onset of a cold winter evening, scuffed with ominous clouds.

Then something moved into view and blocked out the sky. It was the Doctor's face, creased with concern, looking down at her. He was still wearing a spacesuit and helmet, and little lights were flashing inside his collar and reflecting off his nose and cheekbones. The memory of the cliff came suddenly back to Clara; the climb, the earthquake, the fall…

The long fall… to what?

'Am I dead?' she asked. Her voice was a dry croak inside her helmet.

The radio link clicked, and she heard the Doctor's voice say, 'Don't be stupid. Sit up and look around you. Does this look like the afterlife?'

Clara sat up. She was surrounded by whiteness. She was

sitting in deep snow, atop a long drift of snow stretching away to the horizon. In the distance there were grey mountains, and above them empty sky. Clouds drifted across the twilight gloom like long, drawn-out ghosts of the storms she remembered.

There was no cliff. No sign of it at all, not even a heap of rubble, or a vast mound of collapsed granite buried in snow. The nearest mountains were miles away. It looked like she'd woken up in the middle of Antarctica.

'I don't understand.' She climbed unsteadily to her feet. 'Where are we?'

'I don't know for sure.'

'Where's all the snow come from?'

'I don't know.'

'Where's the cliff?'

'Gone.'

It was too much to take in. The whiteness was dazzling her; even though it lacked the harsh reflection of snow on Earth, it was still a contrast to the dismal grey of the planet she had known up to now. She turned around too quickly, trying to find a landmark in the trackless white wasteland, but found only dizziness.

The Doctor grabbed her arm and held her upright. 'You're getting too old for all this, Clara,' he said.

'Shut up before I thump you. Where is everyone?'

'Here and there.'

Gradually, Clara began to see the others, appearing wraithlike out of the whiteness around them. She could see Tibby and Balfour, trudging towards them through the snow. They bent down and helped another spacesuited figure up. Judging by the figure's slightness, Clara guessed it was Jem.

'We ended up quite scattered,' the Doctor said. He held up his left wrist to show a blinking green light set in the control panel. 'I found you by tracking the transponder in your spacesuit.'

Hobbo appeared, taking long, exaggerated steps through the snow. Her face was stony inside her helmet. 'We still can't find Mitch or Tanya,' she said.

'We'll continue the search,' said the Doctor. 'There's enough of us now to spread out a bit and triangulate whatever transponder signals we can pick up.'

The others began to set their radios to scan for the suit transponders. Bewildered and still more dazed than she cared to admit, Clara joined in the search. Tibby and Marco eventually found Mitch and Tanya together, half buried in the snow some two hundred metres away. Tibby knelt down and brushed clumps of snow off Mitch's helmet until they could see his face. Ridiculously, his baseball cap was still firmly jammed on his head.

His immediate reaction was predictable: 'What the hell happened? How did we end up here?'

'Where are we?' Tanya asked as they were helped to their feet. She was physically shaking, but it had to be from shock rather than cold. The survival suits were all compensating for the temperatures, just as Balfour had said they would. Tanya looked around at the vast, snowy scenery. 'Have we been teleported to another world or something?'

'No,' said the Doctor. 'It's the same planet. Same neutron

star, mass, specific gravity, angle and speed of rotation…
They all unequivocally indicate that it is the same planet.'

'But there is some difference in the atmosphere,' said
Balfour. He held up his computer. 'I've been running
checks on air density and content. It's still toxic, so don't
take your helmets off, but it's not as bad as it was before.
A lot more oxygen and nitrogen, a lot less methane… and
this snow is not corrosive, which means that the clouds
are now mostly water rather than acid.'

'Meaning what?' asked Marco with a touch of his
old impatience. 'Can anyone actually explain what just
happened? Why aren't we all dead in a mangled heap of
rock at the bottom of that cliff?'

'We already know the planet is surrounded by discrete
time fields,' the Doctor said. 'There's bound to be
consequences on the surface.'

'Have we travelled in time?' wondered Clara. 'Is that it?'

'Very probably. The earthquake must have been the
result of a massive, localised temporal flux… throwing us
all backwards in time.'

'Backwards?' repeated Marco. 'How can you be sure?
Why not forwards?'

'It's backwards,' said the Doctor. 'Take my word for it. I
can feel it in my bones.'

Marco looked at him scornfully. 'Don't be ridiculous.'

'It's a gift. I can sense time distortion and idiots. There's
one of those looking at me right now.'

Marco turned away with an unhappy grunt. 'Please
yourself.'

'Look around you,' the Doctor told them. He turned

slowly on the spot, arms outstretched. 'We're in the middle of an ice age! The landscape has been carved into pieces by glaciers and the planetary temperature has plummeted to below zero. What should take tens of thousands of years has passed in the time it takes to fall to the ground. It's now a frozen world.'

Clara let her gaze roam across the endless white. She felt she ought to shiver or something, but she was perfectly warm inside her spacesuit. It made the whole thing seem unreal. 'It's like Narnia.'

'Not really,' replied the Doctor matter-of-factly. 'Narnia is a beautiful place. It was only briefly turned into a frozen hell by the despotic witch Jadis.'

She gave him a sideways look. 'I never know when you're joking.'

'I never joke. C. S. Lewis was a personal friend. I'll leave the rest to your imagination.'

She smiled. 'Don't worry, I have a pretty good imagination.'

'That's what he said.'

'But what does it all mean?' asked Tanya.

'It means,' said the Doctor, 'that this strange and dangerous planet has just become infinitely stranger, and infinitely more dangerous.'

'The real question,' said Balfour, 'is what to do now?'

'Find the *Alexandria*,' said Jem. It was the first time she had spoken in quite a while. She didn't make eye contact with any of the others, however, and it almost seemed as though she was speaking to herself.

'There's no reason to believe that it hasn't travelled

back in time with us,' said Balfour. 'It must be around here somewhere.'

'But it could be completely buried under the snow,' said Tibby.

Marco gave a snort of disgust. 'What's the point? It could be anywhere.'

'No, it's quite close by,' said Jem. She held up her arm to show a tiny flashing beacon on her wrist control. 'That's the transponder signal from Dan's spacesuit.'

There was silence. The wind moaned faintly across the wastes.

'Jem, he can't still be alive,' Clara said, as gently as she could. Her voice sounded hollow and unwelcome inside her own helmet. It probably sounded the same way in Jem's.

'I know,' the clone said. 'But he's here somewhere.'

'Which means the *Alexandria* is here too,' said Balfour. The relief was clear in his voice. 'He went down with the ship, so it must be here.'

'Which means the TARDIS will be here as well,' the Doctor confirmed. He was already turning, scanning, looking for any kind of clue in the snow, but there was nothing to see but the empty whiteness.

They walked for hours, using their transceivers to home in on the signal from Dan Laker's spacesuit.

Moving through the snow was exhausting. Each of them was only too aware of how much precious oxygen was being used just to make progress. Heavy clouds the colour of burnished steel were gathering on the horizon, and beneath them swirled a haze of grey. Clara didn't need to be a meteorologist to know that a blizzard was closing in. She trudged on, trying to catch up with the Doctor, who had his sonic screwdriver out and was sweeping it over the snow ahead of them.

'I'm trying to pick up a signal from the TARDIS,' he told Clara when she drew level. The others had spread out in a wide semicircle, checking the readings on their wrist displays. Laker's suit appeared to be sending out a steady pulse and it looked as though they were already heading in the right direction.

Clara looked behind them, studying the advancing storm front. It was catching them up. The clouds were darker, the blizzard less distant.

'How long will our suits keep us warm?' she asked, switching to a private channel with the Doctor.

The Doctor shrugged. 'Long enough. The power cells are small but extremely efficient. They'll last for ever. We'll starve to death long before the thermostats give out.'

'Good to know.'

'Although, to be honest, food isn't the problem. We can survive for quite a long time without eating. Water is another matter.'

'I'm getting thirsty. Everyone must be.'

'The human body is sixty-five per cent water, Clara. Blood, tissues, organs – it's needed everywhere. After just a few days without water, dehydration will increase to the point where the blood will thicken. Your heart will strain to pump it around your body. Your kidneys will fail, your blood pressure will drop. You'll get more and more fatigued and confused. Eventually you'll lapse into a coma. Death will follow quite quickly but it's an agonising way to go.'

'I'm so glad you told me,' Clara said drily.

'It's ironic,' said the Doctor, 'considering we're crossing a wasteland made entirely from water in its frozen state.'

'Ironic, yeah.' If Clara had felt thirsty before, her mouth felt bone dry now. Suddenly she craved a drink, visualising a long, cool carafe of clear water trickling with condensation.

The Doctor continued to scan with the sonic screwdriver. The tip pulsed gently green.

'Any luck with the TARDIS?' Clara asked.

The Doctor stopped and clicked the screwdriver off. 'Nothing at all. It's strange. It should still be with the *Alexandria*. If we can pick up Dan Laker's suit signal, why can't I detect the TARDIS? Unless I'd set the Hostile Action Displacement System, but I don't recall doing that. I'm pretty sure it's broken.'

The Doctor's helmet reflected the snow quite strongly but Clara could still see the look of concern etched into his face. The eyebrows were doing their thing again. 'Should I be worried?'

'We should all be worried, Clara. The time flux we experienced won't be a singular occurrence. If the whole planet is contained within a shifting time field, it will probably happen again, and there's no telling when.'

'So we really need to find the TARDIS urgently.'

'Very urgently, and not just for food and water.'

They plodded on, following the line of spacesuited

figures as they homed in on the tiny transponder signal in another, lost spacesuit. Mitch and Hobbo had forged ahead, wading deep through the snow, carving a trench in which the others could follow a little more easily. Balfour and Tibby were next, with Tanya and Jem following, and then the Doctor and Clara.

Some way behind, as if he was stalking them alone, came Marco.

Clara kept glancing behind to check he was still there. As much as she didn't like him, she would hate for him to become separated. If they lost anyone in this wilderness it could be a disaster. Behind him loomed the towering clouds of the distant snow storm.

'Marco's dropping behind,' she said.

'He wants us all where he can see us,' remarked the Doctor. 'Particularly you and me.'

'He thinks we're keeping something from him – and from the others.'

'Well, we are.'

'Shouldn't we just tell them about the Glamour?'

'No point. They probably wouldn't believe us anyway. The thing with the Glamour is that its influence is utterly insidious, Clara. The person most affected would be the last to realise it.'

Clara thought about this for a moment. 'I don't suppose it would be high on anyone's list of priorities at the moment, anyway.'

'Exactly. They've all got more immediate things to worry about at the moment – like survival. And so have we.'

'Yeah.' Clara looked behind again. Marco was still

trudging after them. It was hard to tell at this distance, but she felt sure his eyes were burning straight into hers.

'*Hey! We've found somethin'!*'

Mitch Keller's voice overrode the private channel, and everybody heard the cry at once and quickened their pace to catch up.

Hobbo was on one knee, studying the lights flashing on her suit's wrist panel. 'It's definitely the captain's suit,' she said. 'Transponder signal's the clearest yet. We're right on top of him.'

Jem got down and started to dig into the snow with shaking hands. Tibby joined her, and soon Mitch and Clara were helping as well. They worked feverishly, scraping away at the snow until they had cleared a ditch half a metre deep. The further down they went the more compact the snow became. Clara began to feel the intense cold through her gloves at last.

But there was no sign of Dan Laker.

Exhausted, Tibby and Clara sat back, panting and dejected. 'He's buried too deep,' said Clara.

'Oh, this is stupid and pointless!' cried Marco angrily. He turned and kicked at the snow, sending lumps of it exploding through the air. 'We're all going to die here and—'

'Wait,' said Jem. She was the only one still digging, scraping away at the bottom of the ditch like a dog looking for a bone. 'He's here.'

Jem cleared away a patch of snow to reveal a flash of blue. She worked until there was more blue visible, the clear metallic blue of the *Alexandria* spacesuits and the helmet tag which said 'LAKER', and then they all fell to their knees and worked with Jem until they had dug the body free of its deep white grave.

Clara had worried that Laker might have been crushed in the wreckage of the ship but the suit had done its job well and survived intact. The little beacon on the wrist panel gently pulsed, the slow and steady heartbeat of death.

'The suit's still sealed,' reported Hobbo, checking the display. 'No loss of integrity.'

Jem's voice was small but clear in everyone's helmet: 'Could he still be…?'

Laker's own helmet was masked with a layer of frost. Mitch Keller leaned forward and scraped at the curved surface, scratching through the crystallised glaze until the clear transparency of the chain glass was revealed. Seconds later they could see into Laker's helmet, and Jem's hand flew to her mouth.

Brittle strands of hair clung to shrivelled skin. The eyes were dry and sunken, with a ragged hole beneath them where the nose should have been and dark, crumbling teeth exposed between withered lips.

It was the face of a thousand-year-old corpse.

Chapter
12

Clara was reminded of an Egyptian mummy she had once seen on a museum visit. Laker had the same stiff, papery look, but this was worse because she had known this man as a living person and she could still see a grim likeness in the desiccated features that remained. The sight also brought back discomforting memories of a trip on the Orient Express, and a different kind of mummy that was anything but dead.

Jem remained kneeling, completely silent, unable to tear her gaze away from the corpse.

Mitch Keller climbed slowly to his feet, weighed down with sadness. Hobbo stood up as well, and turned away. Tibby Vent looked as though she wanted to be sick; her face was nearly as pale as Jem's.

'What's happened to him?' asked Clara.

'He must have been caught on the very edge of the time flux,' said the Doctor. 'It looks as though his suit might have been all right but the organic contents have been aged to death – and beyond.'

Clara felt a sudden flash of irritation. 'Organic contents?'

'That was a human being,' said Tanya Flexx quietly. 'A *person.*'

'And as such he was made of organic matter,' the Doctor said. 'The result is the same.'

Tanya simply turned and walked away. Clara felt tears stinging in her eyes. She fiddled with the controls on her wrist and selected the private channel to speak to the Doctor. 'I thought maybe…' she started to say, but then choked a little. 'I hoped that somehow…'

'He was dead the moment he went over the cliff, Clara,' the Doctor said softly.

She sniffed. 'Why are you being so cold? I know you're not human, but…'

'We're running out of time, Clara. Our oxygen levels are getting dangerously low. We need to get to the TARDIS, and this is just slowing us down.'

Clara turned to look at him, but his face was a cold mask, his eyes hard and distant. He could be like that, sometimes. 'They're grieving,' she said.

'Are you grieving?'

'I'm upset. He was a good man, a decent man, and he didn't deserve this. Nor did Jem.'

'And yet it still happened. The universe has no respect for people or relationships, Clara. You of all people should know that.'

'It doesn't mean we have to stop caring. Or is that what you've done now? Stopped caring?'

The Doctor's eyes focused on Clara's. There was a dark, timeless fatigue in them sometimes that she only glimpsed occasionally. For most of the time he kept it hidden, but now she could see it all: two thousand years of lost friends and loved ones. 'No, I've not stopped caring. I never stop caring. But right now I have to care for the living, Clara. We have to carry on without Laker if we're not going to end up joining him.'

Mitch walked around the body and put a hand on Jem's shoulder. 'We'll bury him.'

'What about the suit?' asked Hobbo. 'It's still functional.'

'It's what kept him like he is,' the Doctor said. 'Without it he would probably turn to dust.'

They all thought about this for a moment but no one offered any further suggestions.

'Jem?' said Mitch eventually.

'I can't leave him like this,' Jem replied. 'It's just… horrible.'

'Whatever you do, it must be soon,' said the Doctor. 'We're getting low on oxygen, and we don't know how much longer it will take to find the TARDIS. There's also the possibility of another time flux. It could happen again at any moment.'

Mitch shook his head. 'I don't care. I ain't leavin' Dan like this. We have to bury him.'

'Switch off the suit first.' This was from Jem. She still hadn't moved, she still had one hand resting on Laker's space helmet.

After a pause, Mitch asked, 'Who's gonna do that?'

'I will,' said Marco Spritt. It was the first time he'd spoken since they had discovered Laker's body, and he said it with such conviction that it was clear he was impatient to move on.

Mitch looked fiercely at Marco and balled his fists, but Jem shook her head. 'No. It should be me.'

She leaned over Laker's body, touching the spacesuit and helmet lovingly. It was as close to him as she could get now. She bent low and whispered her farewells. 'My pilot, my captain. I love you.'

In silence, she felt for the suit's control panel and slowly, deliberately went through the sequence that would deactivate the life-support system. Alarm indicators flashed brilliantly but she ignored them. Clara had to look away. The suit slowly powered down and the lights blinked off one by one. Eventually the illumination in the helmet faded.

'I thought you said he'd turn to dust,' Clara said on her private channel to the Doctor.

'Not immediately. But switching off the life support will speed up the process.'

They buried Laker's body in the snow. In some ways it felt like they were just putting him back where they'd found him, but this time they had all – Jem especially – been able to say a proper goodbye.

'It probably falls to me to say a few words now,' said Balfour. He took a deep breath. 'The truth is, I don't know what to say. This started out as an adventure… only now it feels more like a nightmare. Dan Laker was a good man, maybe even the best of us. He's been taken too soon – not just from us, and Jem, but from the universe. May his soul rest in peace.'

They stood in a circle around the icy grave for a few more minutes before they each agreed it was time to move on. A brisk wind had come up from across the wastes, the cold breath of the approaching storm, bringing the first squalls of the blizzard with it. Soon the place where Dan Laker had been buried would be invisible again.

'I think I've got a signal from the TARDIS,' said the Doctor. He'd raised his voice because the wind was howling now, but Clara could hear him clearly over the radio link. The sky above them was dark with cloud and the blizzard was building up. She wiped her helmet visor for the umpteenth time so that she could see the Doctor properly. He was holding his sonic screwdriver up in front of his face, peering at it closely, tilting it this way and that. The light pulsed green, and Clara could hear the faint bleeping noise through her audio pick-up. 'It's weak, but it's definitely there,' the Doctor added. He couldn't keep the excitement out of his voice and he quickened his pace through the snow. 'It's the TARDIS!'

Clara stomped through the blizzard after him. If she let him get too far ahead, she wouldn't be able to see him at all. Her boots were covered in thick clumps of snow and she was getting tired. Her mouth was parched. She checked her oxygen level every few minutes. It was bad enough measuring out your remaining life as a matter of hours; worse still when you had an actual countdown on your wrist.

'I can't see anything,' she said. Her voice came out in a ragged pant.

'I've extended the screwdriver's scanning capability to beyond spatial coordinates,' the Doctor said.

'Do I really want to know what that means?'

'It means the TARDIS could well be around here somewhere,' the Doctor said, turning in a circle as he walked, 'but in another time period.'

'Awkward, then.'

The Doctor came to a halt, checked the screwdriver again, and then stood with his legs apart and his hands on his hips. The snow flurried around him. 'Well, here we are.'

The rest of the party caught up after a minute or two. Jem, Tibby and Balfour, with Mitch, Hobbo, Tanya and Marco bringing up the rear. None of them had talked much since Laker's funeral, and it wasn't simply out of respect. The fact was they were all tired and thirsty. Jem and Mitch were suffering particularly, and they sat down slowly in the snow.

'I don't know how much longer I can keep this pace up,' Jem confessed.

'You just need a rest, sweetheart,' Tanya told her. 'We all do.'

'I need about minus thirty years,' grumbled Mitch.

Raymond Balfour trudged through the snow to join the Doctor and Clara. 'How much further, Doctor?'

'Not much further.' The Doctor seemed more interested in his sonic screwdriver, clicking through a number of different settings and testing the result.

Clara tapped the Doctor on the shoulder. 'You said, "Here we are." Where's the TARDIS?'

'It's here,' the Doctor replied, busily adjusting the screwdriver. 'Just not at the moment.'

'Which moment will it be here, then? I'm hoping for "in the next few".'

More fiddling with the sonic screwdriver. 'Impossible to say, I'm afraid.'

'I thought you said the TARDIS was our only hope?'

'It is.'

'Are you aware of the same flaw in your plan as I am?'

'And what flaw would that be?'

'That if we're in the right place for the TARDIS, but not the right time, then it's as good as not here at all.'

'That's not a flaw. It's an inconvenience.' The Doctor continued to fiddle with the screwdriver.

Clara sighed and walked away, astonished by how disappointed she felt. Not so much disappointed in the situation, but disappointed with the Doctor. He usually solved problems like this. He might be brusque, even rude, and infuriatingly unpredictable, but he always found a way. Clara felt as if she had no more tears to cry, and her heart burned with frustration.

The snow was drifting up in a slope ahead of her. She carried on regardless, taking long, exaggerated steps. Her legs sank almost up to her knees with every stride. Eventually she reached the top of the rise and looked to see what lay beyond it. A part of her mind thought she might catch a glimpse of blue in the swirling blizzard, the faint square shape of an old police box, half buried by the snowstorm, waiting for them, but just hidden from view.

But the TARDIS wasn't there.

What was there was a great, black crack in the snow which swallowed up the dancing flakes like a vast, hungry mouth.

'Come and look at this!' she called. The radio link carried

her voice perfectly well, so there was no need to shout, but she couldn't help it.

Mitch, Hobbo and the Doctor clambered up the slope after her.

'Another cliff?' said Hobbo miserably.

'It's the edge of the glacier,' said the Doctor.

They looked down into the vast grey chasm. They couldn't see the bottom; it was lost in the white squall. But the edges of the crack were sheer, translucent ice, streaked with dark sediment.

'You'd need specialist equipment to get down there,' said Mitch.

'Which we don't have,' said Hobbo.

'No.'

It wasn't like the cliff. That had been a rough, rugged tear in the rocky landscape with plenty of handholds and footholds and ledges and narrow, zigzagging paths. This was nothing but sheer ice. It would take a team of experienced mountaineers equipped with ropes, ice-picks and crampons to even consider a climb.

'Is the TARDIS down there?' Clara asked, her voice shaking. 'Please tell me it isn't.'

The Doctor pointed the sonic screwdriver into the frozen maw and took a reading. 'No, it isn't,' he said.

'You're lying, aren't you?'

The Doctor sighed and closed the screwdriver with a decisive click. 'Yes. I'm lying. It's down there.'

They waded back down the slope. Clara could feel her heart pounding with the exertion now and wondered how much oxygen she was using up. Mitch Keller looked exhausted; he wasn't a young man by any means, but he still wasn't making as much fuss as Marco Spritt, who was less than half his age.

'This is madness,' Marco said. 'We're walking to nowhere. We're all going to die!'

'That's enough of that, Marco,' warned Tanya.

'No one wants to hear your opinion,' added Jem. 'Can't you see we're all trying to deal with this as well? Not just you?' She was close to tears.

Tanya put an arm around her shoulders and said, 'Take it easy, sweetheart. He's not worth it.'

'Pah,' Marco said, kicking at the snow.

Jem sank to her knees, holding her helmet. 'I'm sorry. It's just that my head hurts so much…'

'You've been under a lot of strain,' Tanya said.

'No, it's not that. This is something different. This is like in the wormhole. Movements in the dark matter… voices calling for me.'

'What is it?' asked the Doctor.

'There's someone coming. Or *something*. Look!' Jem pointed into the swirling snow, but it was impossible make out anything other than a white haze.

'She's starting to hallucinate,' said Tanya. 'She's weak. Upset. She's seeing things.'

'No,' Clara said. 'She isn't. Look.'

In the mist of snow, Clara could see shapes moving towards them. Tall, dark shapes rendered almost invisible by the blizzard. Instinctively, the group drew closer together.

The snow seemed to move around them, churning and throwing up a white fog which was caught by the wind and swirled around them like sheets. The dark figures loomed through the whiteout, ghostly and silent. A coruscating blue glow surrounded them like a gas flame.

'What are they?'

Suddenly Clara was sliding downwards, as if a hole had opened up in the snowdrift and she was falling into it. She put her hand out to balance and saw that the others were all toppling over as well, as the snow beneath their feet began to fall away like sand in an egg timer. She looked up at the approaching ghosts, saw a glimpse of long, dark faces beneath deep hoods, and then lost sight of everything as the snow rose up around her.

She heard her helmet radio crackle and the Doctor's voice: 'Temporal flux! It's happening again!'

And then the world dissolved around her in a grey maelstrom, streaked with sudden bands of colour and light, flickering faster and faster until she could see nothing but a blur of movement. She reached out again, and to her great surprise caught hold of someone else's outstretched hand. She pulled them closer, clung on to them, and they grabbed hold of Clara in return. Together they fell without even moving, until eventually the dazzling sense of movement became too great and Clara had to close her eyes.

Chapter

13

After the blank whiteness of the ice age, the sudden green of the jungle was almost overwhelming.

It was dark and verdant, an insane tangle of branches in every direction. Clara felt trapped; the vegetation was oppressively close, almost impenetrable. Creepers festooned with tendrils of long, parasitic weed dangled from a dense canopy of branches stretching up as far as she could see. A dim light filtered down through layers of tangled leaves and knotted vines.

Violently coloured blooms – they were all deep purple and blood red – sprouted aggressive-looking stamen barbed with sharp yellow seeds. Insects the size of rodents crawled everywhere, bristling with legs and wings and wavering antennae.

There was no sign of any other human being. Clara couldn't even see the forest floor; she was sprawled across thick, intertwined boughs covered in moss. More twisting branches, wreathed with a tangle of growth that could have been the beginnings of roots or just more branches, lay below.

'Hello?' she called. She checked that her helmet communicator was switched to the shared channel and called again. 'Doctor? Tibby? Mitch…? Anyone at all?'

There was no reply. She listened carefully, switched her receiver to external audio. She could hear all the sounds of jungle life – a constant rustling, clicking, chirping, hooting… but no human signs at all.

She tried the Doctor's private channel, but there was no response from that either. There was no response on any channel. A flashing light on her wrist panel caught her attention, and with a shock she saw that her oxygen levels were dangerously low. She was down to less than an hour's air left. She must have been unconscious for quite a while. A sudden panic filled her as she thought the others, unable to find her in the jungle, might have moved on without her.

Clara tried to keep her pulse rate steady and her breathing even. She forced herself to rationalise the situation, examine what had happened. She remembered the Doctor saying that another time flux was taking place, as the arctic conditions blurred and changed and then she couldn't recall much else. Obviously she had travelled in time again, to another epoch, where the planet was covered with lush green vegetation. Probably it was the equivalent of prehistoric Earth. Perhaps there were even dinosaurs here.

None of this was actually helping. In fact, she was frightening herself even more.

Clara crawled along the branch until she reached what looked like the trunk of whatever giant tree she was in. The bark was covered with a thick, slippery moss full of flies. Trusting her spacesuit to protect her, she began to climb carefully down the tree.

Clara glimpsed a familiar, metallic blue colour below and felt a surge of hope. She climbed rapidly down and found a man in an *Alexandria* spacesuit slumped over a thick branch, half hidden by long, spiky leaves. She clambered around him and until she could see it was Raymond Balfour, completely unconscious. She rapped a knuckle on the helmet and, to her immense relief, Balfour opened his eyes.

'Miss Oswald?' He turned over and sat up groggily. He looked around in amazement.

'I know,' said Clara. 'Jungle.' But she couldn't help smiling. She'd found someone else alive at least.

'Where's everyone else?' Balfour asked. 'Where's Tibby?'

'I don't know. You're the first I've found.'

Balfour's face looked grim. Or was it simply determined? Clara couldn't see any of the enthusiastic amateur explorer he wanted to be. All she could see now was a survivor.

'Come on,' he said. 'We need to find the others.'

Balfour surprised Clara. He accepted the change of scene more easily than she would have guessed, and in fact seemed almost resigned to their predicament. He also thought of something that Clara had not, and she could have kicked herself: scanning for the signals of any other spacesuit transponders in the area. They picked up two clear signals, from Tibby Vent and Tanya Flexx. There was nothing for any of the others.

While they were planning how to coordinate a search, and how best to triangulate on each of the signals they had, the foliage started to rustle violently behind them. They whirled around, expected some kind of jungle predator, but there was nothing – until a thick curtain of vines was torn away to reveal two figures in *Alexandria* spacesuits.

'Thank god we've found you,' gasped Tanya.

Tibby was almost crying with relief. 'We only just picked up your suit signals.'

'Thank goodness you're all right,' said Balfour.

'Took us twenty minutes to get through the jungle,' Tanya said.

'The signal range must be affected by the trees,' Balfour surmised. 'It's playing havoc with the radios, too. But the others could be here somewhere; we just can't track them.'

Hugs were exchanged, made awkward by the suits and helmets, but in truth it felt like there was little to celebrate. Clara tried repeatedly to locate the Doctor's transponder, or contact him via the radio, but there was nothing.

'So what now?' asked Balfour.

'I suggest we find a good hotel and book in for the night,' said Tanya. 'I for one could do with a long soak in a hot tub.'

They smiled dutifully but they were all too aware of the seriousness of their position.

'I don't know about you, but I'm getting really low on oxygen,' said Tibby. She held up her wrist so that they could see the flashing light.

A long scream tore through the jungle and they all whirled to face the direction it came from.

'What the hell?' Tanya stood up. 'That sounded almost human to me.'

Another scream. 'Help me! Oh, for pity's sake, help me!'

'All too human,' said Clara, moving towards the sound.

They followed the noise for a short distance, climbing down ten metres through the branches until they reached a matted tangle of undergrowth covering a long, wide bough. Long, sharp spikes of some horn-like material protruded from the undergrowth, reaching up into the fetid air like jagged knives. Next to them lay a man in a spacesuit, on his back, yelling and flailing his arms in the air.

'It's OK, Marco,' said Clara. 'We're here. Calm down or you're going to waste what's left of your oxygen.'

Marco scrabbled into a sitting position. Inside his helmet his face was a twisted mask of pain and terror. His gloved hands were scratching at the visor. 'I've got no oxygen! It's all gone! The air's all gone! My helmet's cracked! Oh, for pity's sake help me!'

They checked his helmet and Balfour quickly found a narrow gap in the glass and a series of small cracks. 'These are supposed to be indestructible,' he muttered, with the air of a man who'd paid a lot of money and not got what he expected.

'Almost indestructible,' said Clara. 'Maybe it was weakened by the acid rain.'

'He must have hit one of these spikes,' Balfour said. 'It's cracked the visor and broke the transponder and radio.'

'I've lost all my oxygen!' wept Marco. He shook his wrist at them to show the air indicator. It was glowing a solid red. Empty.

'And yet,' said Clara, 'you're still breathing.'

'And yelling,' added Tibby.

'You're lucky those spikes only cracked your helmet,' said Tanya. 'A bit further to your left and they would have gone straight through you.'

Marco gazed at the carpet of spikes and turned pale. Gradually he began to calm down.

'The air here must be breathable, though,' Clara realised.

They looked at each other, hope suddenly rising inside. Balfour ran a check on his suit diagnostic panel. 'Scanning now. Mainly nitrogen… fair amount of oxygen…'

Tanya was already reaching up for her helmet seal. She didn't wait for a full analysis. She unlatched the helmet and tore it off with a gasp of relief, her black hair falling in a tumble around her head. She took in a long, deep breath and then slowly exhaled.

Clara, Tibby and Balfour watched her closely.

'Oh, that is good,' Tanya said, closing her eyes. She breathed deeply. 'Boy, could I do with a drink just now.'

'If there's air here then there might be water,' said Tibby.

'Never mind about that,' said Marco Spritt. He got to his feet, shaking his arm free from Clara. He fiddled with the latches on his broken helmet and took it off. 'I could have suffocated. I might have died!'

'But you didn't,' Balfour said.

'The helmet was faulty,' Marco said. He threw it violently away into the jungle. 'I'm holding you responsible for that, Balfour.'

'Hey,' said Clara. 'Stop being so ungrateful. It was the acid.'

'Ungrateful? There's nothing to be grateful for! And where the hell are we, anyway?'

Clara took off her own helmet. The air was warm and humid and full of the rank stench of rotting vegetation, but it felt like the most beautiful air she had ever breathed.

Tibby and Balfour took off theirs too and for a minute the four of them just stood and breathed.

'I don't know about you lot but I'm sweating like a pig in this suit,' said Tanya. She unsealed the steelex and then quickly pulled the whole suit off, before anyone had a chance to protest.

'Maybe we should keep them on… just to be safe,' suggested Tibby.

'Safe?' Marco snorted. 'We haven't been safe since we came out of the wormhole!'

'There could be another time flux,' Clara said. 'We don't know where we'll end up, or what the conditions would be.'

Tanya didn't seemed concerned. 'Suit's not much use if there's no air in the tank,' she said as she screwed the steelex material up into a ball and shoved it inside her helmet. Then she dropped the helmet on the ground and stretched like a cat. 'Ye gods, but I'm tired.'

'Can't we replenish the oxygen tanks from the air?' Clara asked.

'No,' Marco said bitterly. 'They use solid-state oxygen. Can't be done.'

'I don't really understand any of this,' said Tibby. 'Snow one minute, jungle the next… What's going on?'

'The Doctor said we were dropping back through time,'

Clara said. 'Millions of years, maybe, slipping through various eras in the planet's past. This could be prehistoric, before it was all destroyed by the ice age.'

'And it could happen again?'

'Yes. Any time.'

'Where is the Doctor, though?' asked Balfour. 'And Mitch and Hobbo and Jem? They must be here somewhere…'

'I hope so,' Clara said. She could feel the perspiration all over her body, seeping its way into every part of her spacesuit. Tanya was right; it was getting uncomfortable, especially wearing their own clothes under the suits. With the helmets on and sealed, the suit thermostats had kept them warm in the snow and cool in the jungle. But without them they were unprotected.

'Hey, look what I've found!' Tanya's voice drifted back through the undergrowth.

Clara felt a flash of worry. 'We should stick together,' she said, as they climbed through the foliage to find Tanya. She wanted to organise a search for the Doctor and the others, and this was just a distraction.

Tanya had found a pool. It looked like clear water, rain water perhaps, gathered in a shallow dip in one of the broad branches of the trees. There were a number of pools where the water had gathered in deep gouges in the bark. Thick, rubbery leaves formed a low ceiling over the area, draping it in shade. It felt marginally cooler here but there was a strange, fetid smell. Around the edge where a number of dark, mustard-yellow blooms speckled with black patches.

'Not deep enough for a bath,' Tanya said, bending down

to look into the nearest pool. 'But I'm not complaining.'

'It might not be safe to drink,' Clara warned, although her mouth was tingling with the prospect. 'It could still be full of acid.'

'How do you even know it's water?' asked Marco crossly. 'You should check it first.'

'You're right,' said Clara. She turned to Balfour. 'Can we do some sort of test? Check whether it's water or not?'

'What's this?' asked Tibby, examining the blooms growing around the edge of the area. The mustard-coloured petals were thick, fibrous hand-shapes cupping a deep, dark centre. Each of them was full of something that looked like tar, but there were bubbles floating on the surface.

'Looks a bit like frogspawn,' said Clara. 'Only it's black.' She didn't like it. It looked as if something was concealed beneath the surface, quietly seething, waiting. And the smell was very odd; meaty and threatening. It made her nose wrinkle, and she was worried the others were getting too close. 'Maybe we should stay away from them,' she advised.

'There's more over here,' said Tanya. 'In fact all the plants are full of this stuff...'

There was a noise like a sneeze and one of the plants suddenly closed up, the petals snapping shut like a Venus Fly Trap. The black goo inside sprayed all over Tanya and she staggered back with a cry.

'Get away from it!' Clara yelled, but it was too late. Tanya's bare arms and shoulders were spattered with the tar-like substance.

They pulled her away from the plants, stumbling back through the undergrowth until they were clear of the area.

'It's stinging,' Tanya gasped.

Balfour tried to get some of the dark slime off her arms, wiping at it with his spacesuit gloves still on, but the goo was thick and seemed to have stuck to the skin.

'Find somewhere for her to sit,' Clara said. Tibby and Balfour helped Tanya back the way they'd come, with Marco clearing a rough path through the foliage.

They sat Tanya down against the bole of a tree. The frogspawn seemed to be spreading, thinning out as it expanded. Some of the larger patches were already joining up.

'Should've kept my suit on,' Tanya said. Her arms, shoulders and part of her neck were covered in the tar. As they watched, it spread further, oozing slowly over her flesh.

'There must be something we can do!' Tibby looked desperately at the others.

'It's quite interesting, I suppose,' Tanya said. She winced, clearly in pain, and struggled to continue. 'I'm an exobiologist, after all, as well as a medic. You were right, Clara – it's like frogspawn; some kind of amniotic fluid containing eggs.' She held up her left arm, which was now almost completely covered. 'You can see them as it moves, like tiny little balls in the slime.'

'It's disgusting,' said Marco.

'But why did the plant spray it over you?' asked Balfour.

'What does all life need to thrive?' Tanya asked him.

'Food. Protein. I must've looked like a good bet.'

The black spawn had spread further as she spoke, oozing up her neck and towards her face.

'What can we do?' asked Clara, feeling sick with helplessness. 'Can't we try to wash it off... use the water?'

'We can't be sure the water is safe,' Balfour objected. 'If it even is water.'

'But there must be something we can do!'

'Very little, actually.' Tanya grimaced, clearly in pain as the blackness spread. It was slowly becoming one solid layer. 'Cell duplication is happening at a tremendous rate,' she noted. 'Wow.'

It rose further up her neck, over her chin. She pressed her lips shut as it approached her mouth. The others watched in horror as the tar flowed over her mouth, sealing it shut. Her nostrils were flaring in panic. Her eyes widened in fear and pain as, with abominable speed, the spawn enveloped her head, closing over her nose and eyes, as if her face was disappearing beneath the surface of a pool of ink.

'It's killing her!' Marco said.

The entire upper half of Tanya's body was now covered in a film of black spawn. She struggled weakly, and then stopped moving altogether. Her legs twitched once and then lay still.

Tibby covered her face with her hands, unable to look. Balfour put his arm around her, pulled her away from the scene.

Clara, numb with revulsion, couldn't tear her gaze away. The glistening black shape of Tanya had begun to lose definition, the nose flattening, her head compressing, arms drawing in across the body as the spawn contracted, or consumed, what it contained. The spawn oozed and pulsed, hard pustules growing out of the surface – little eggs, perhaps, ready to hatch.

'It happened so quickly,' said Balfour, in a disbelieving whisper. 'I can hardly believe it.'

Tibby was sobbing. 'There was nothing we could do… nothing…'

'We've got to get away from here,' Clara said, standing up.

'That's wonderful advice,' Marco sneered. He gestured to the thick jungle surrounded them. 'But where exactly do you suggest we go?'

Chapter

14

The Doctor stood on a metal wall overlooking a dark, craggy landscape swathed in mist.

The sky was as black as dried blood; what passed for night on this world of neutron dusk. He could see the land around him because the soil appeared to contain some kind of slow-decay isotope that imbued it with the faint radiance of putrefying meat. He could breathe the air because the latest time flux had carried him to some distant epoch in the planet's long history when nitrogen and oxygen were the primary gases making up the atmosphere. He sniffed, lifting his long, aquiline nose to trace a particular scent he couldn't quite place. Ozone? Cordite? He sniffed again, but it was gone. It was as if the luminescent ground had somehow absorbed the odours of a battlefield from a hundred thousand years before.

'Any sign?' asked Mitch Keller, climbing up onto the wall next to him. His baseball cap was pulled firmly down, his ship overalls crumpled and dirt-smeared. Like the Doctor, he had removed his spacesuit. They'd run out of air anyway and the suits had quickly become an encumbrance.

'Nothing,' said the Doctor. He had been scanning the area from this vantage point, looking for Clara and the others. In the distance they could see the hazy orange fire of volcanoes. Perhaps it was the sulphurous fumes, borne on the wind, that he could smell.

'They must be around here somewhere,' Mitch said. He looked back into the crumbling ruins behind them, where Hobbo was sitting with Jem. Mist, illuminated by the soft glow of the earth, coiled slowly around their feet.

The Doctor looked sceptical. 'The time fluxes are unpredictable at best, but something's brought us back in time, further than ever. We've been separated from the others and I've no idea why.'

'You make it sound like it's deliberate.'

'I'm beginning to think it is. There's an intelligence at work here – something with a purpose. I just don't know what it is yet. As for Clara and the others, well, they could be anywhere… and any when.'

Mitch scratched the stubble on his chin. 'I just hope they're all still together.'

'We've all stayed together; there's no reason why they shouldn't.'

If Mitch thought the Doctor was just trying to sound positive and keep his hopes up, he didn't say anything. He watched the Doctor take out his sonic screwdriver and switch it on. The green light blinked rhythmically.

'The TARDIS?' asked Mitch.

'It's distant in terms of time rather than space. But we're closer than before.' The Doctor shut the screwdriver down. 'At least the time fluxes are taking us in the right direction chronologically. The problem is that the signal itself is getting weaker. We have to find it soon or else we might lose it altogether.'

'At least we can breathe now.'

'True. But we're still going to need food and water. I can't see much of either here, can you?'

Mitch didn't reply. He didn't need to. The land they were in was as barren as any they could imagine – miles of trackless fog and decaying ruins. Long ago, there must have been some sort of civilisation here. Left behind were the remnants of its existence: a corroded metal city made of rust-crumbled walls, exposed basements, the broken stubs of what might have been towers or gantries. There was nothing but sharp metallic edges, cracked and shot through with rust and lichen.

'Who d'you reckon lived here?' Mitch wondered.

'I don't think anyone ever lived here,' replied the Doctor. 'I think it was built and abandoned before it was used. Perhaps it was the result of some kind of automated construction that was forgotten about, or just never needed.'

'Mechonoids, you mean?'

'Something like that, perhaps. Whatever it was, no one came. The place was left derelict. The elements moved in – the wind and the rain, the fog. It's had a corrosive effect over thousands of years.'

'And the ghosts?'

They'd seen them moving in the ruins: not just the local wildlife, which seemed to be some kind of predator insect that had been stalking them since their arrival, but spectral figures half-glimpsed through the ragged gaps or crumbling doorways. The visions were always fleeting.

The Doctor's eyes narrowed, his brows drawing down like a hood over his thoughts. 'Now they are interesting,' he admitted. 'Could they be the intelligence at work here, I wonder?'

'Look,' said Mitch, pointing across the remains. Two or three hundred metres away there was a soft, blue light. After a moment, a tall, spectral figure seemed to glide through the walkway, slowly turning this way and that before gradually fading into the mist. 'Another one.'

'We saw the same sort of thing in the ice age, remember, just before the time flux,' noted the Doctor. 'But who are they? What do they want?'

'You believe in ghosts, Doc? Maybe this place *was* inhabited. Maybe these are the ghosts of the people who lived here.'

'I doubt that. They're too tall for the architecture, for one thing. And as I said, there's nothing left here to indicate that there was any intelligent life at all. No, they're visitors here, Mitch – just like us.'

Another ghost appeared, a pallid figure drifting silently through the ruins on some unknown errand. Mitch shivered. 'They still give me the creeps.'

Hobbo clambered up the wall to join them. 'More ghosts an' ghouls?' she asked as they watched the glow fade.

'They're appearing more frequently now,' said the Doctor thoughtfully. 'We must be closing in on the epicentre of the time flux.'

'We can't stay where we are, though,' said Hobbo. 'Jem's

still in shock but those predators are closin' in.'

The predator insects had been roaming the area since they arrived, scuttling around the darker corners of the ruins, hiding in the shadows on top of the walls where the ground light couldn't reach them. According to the Doctor they were evolutionary misfires, typical of experimental prehistoric life. But they were hunters nevertheless; a pack of them had turned on one of their own, dismembering and devouring it with brutal efficiency. Now they seemed to be circling the Doctor and his party through the fog, getting closer all the time.

'They look for the weakest,' Hobbo said. 'That's what predators do, isn't it? Stalk their prey and pick off the weakest.'

Even though Mitch was an old man, they all knew she was referring to Jem. The clone astrogator was alone, depressed, consumed with grief. It was almost like she'd given up. She was exhausted and an obvious target for any hunter.

'Come on,' said Mitch. 'Let's move out.'

The Doctor and Mitch went ahead while Hobbo helped Jem along. They were heading away from the predators, deeper into the ruins.

The Doctor came to a sudden stop as a faint blue glow appeared around the corner ahead of them. The group drew together as the apparition approached – a tall, hooded figure which loomed over them, casting a strange light across the ruins. Shadows seemed to crawl away from it to hide in the mist.

'Everybody remain calm,' said the Doctor. He stood up straight and faced the ghost directly as it approached. Inside the hood, just visible within the ghastly light, was a long, birdlike face with dark eyes.

And then it disappeared, like smoke on the breeze.

'They're really very irritating,' grumbled the Doctor. 'Coming and going like that without saying a word. Who do they think they are?'

'The Phaeron,' said Jem.

They all turned to look at her.

'I can sense them,' she explained. 'It's just like when I was on the *Alexandria*, coming through the wormhole.'

'You mean the voices? You said you heard voices again. You could sense the fluctuations in dark matter.'

Jem frowned. 'Something like that. It's just a feeling. But they are the Phaeron – or the ghosts of the Phaeron. I'm sure of it.'

'Then why don't they introduce themselves?' asked Mitch. 'Instead of just creepin' around all the time?'

'Maybe they are trying to,' said Jem.

'Perhaps they can't even see us,' suggested the Doctor as he examined the spot where the wraith had passed moments before. The glowing dust was undisturbed by its passing, as if it had never been there at all. His fists clenched and unclenched as he thought. 'Or perhaps they only perceive us faintly, as ghosts of ourselves, in whatever time stream they exist.'

They had paused for too long. Something scrambled up onto the top of the nearest wall with long, skittering legs. A multitude of glistening, egg-like eyes focused on the intruders and the insect distended its wide, hooked jaws to let out a sharp screech of triumph.

Hobbo grabbed Jem and pulled her out of the way as the insect ran straight down the wall. Its mandibles snapped at the air where Jem had stood a moment before. It threw back its thin head and its black mouth gaped open, full of concentric rings of sharp, hooked fangs. It screeched again, sending a thin spray of saliva into the cold night air.

'When I say run…' said the Doctor quietly, but Hobbo had already grabbed Jem's hand and pulled her away, further into the ruins. The Doctor took hold of Mitch's arm and propelled him bodily after them.

More of the insectoid creatures were climbing up the walls to join the first, waving their antennae in the night air and letting out a series of blood-curdling shrieks. The hunt was on.

Jem was struggling to keep up. She was panting by the time they reached a wide, central plaza. Moss grew up a series of wide, cylindrical columns but whatever kind of roof they had once supported was long gone. Above was nothing but empty black space. Around them was the slowly rolling fog, and the predators. They could all hear them – scuttling through the mist, unseen but ever present.

'Don't they ever give up?' Hobbo wondered bitterly.

'It's not in their nature,' said the Doctor. 'They'll already have marked one of us off as prey. Now they're just herding us, and waiting for the opportunity to strike.'

They crossed the open plaza, footsteps echoing around the columns and colonnades. The walls were even more bent and broken here, little more than misshapen lumps of corroded iron covered in a layer of fibrous grey lichen. There was no straight route through – they had to climb over slabs of fallen debris wherever they could.

'This ain't good,' said Mitch, helping Jem over one large boulder. 'We're vulnerable.'

'We're vulnerable anywhere,' said the Doctor.

'You sure this is the right way?' asked Hobbo.

The Doctor was scanning with his sonic screwdriver, trying to pick up the faintest signal. 'We need to get as close to the TARDIS as possible, at least in space. Then – well, it's just a matter of time, I'm afraid.'

Dark shapes crawled through the fog around them, slipping in between the broken metalwork, working their way closer and closer.

'I think they're gettin' ready to attack,' whispered Hobbo, walking backwards so that she could keep an eye on the predators.

'Now would be the perfect time,' admitted the Doctor, turning around in a circle to see how many there were. He counted a dozen that he could see; there were probably more hidden in the fog. 'We can't move quickly and they've got us surrounded.'

'Gotta keep movin',' advised Mitch. 'If we stop they'll know we're finished.'

'Protect Jem,' said the Doctor. 'It'll be her they're after.'

'No, wait,' Jem said. They paused, looking all around them. The mist was closing in. Sharp spires rose irregularly from the milky vapour, some of them connected by rusting gantries and angular fingers of metal poking out like aerials. 'Whatever this place is,' Jem said, 'the Phaeron must be here for a reason. And they've brought us here, too. I can sense that now, in the same way I sensed them in the wormhole. They're connected somehow.'

'With the wormhole?' The Doctor's frown deepened. 'Is that even possible?'

'It must be. It's the only way I could have heard them then. It's the only way I can hear them now.' Jem held her head in both hands, rubbing gently at the scalp and its lattice of augmentation sockets. 'It's the same thing, the same whispers in the dark matter. The imperfection. They keep talking about an imperfection.'

'Do we have to discuss this now?' asked Mitch nervously.

'Wait,' said the Doctor. 'If what Jem says is true, then the situation is more serious than I thought. And I already thought it was very, very serious indeed.' The look of deep concern on his long, lined features suddenly morphed into a brighter one as he took a sharp intake of breath. 'Oh! Oh, I've just had the most extraordinary thought! What if the Phaeron are *made* of dark matter? Oh, that would be extraordinary! That would be something *completely new*, and completely different – like nothing I've ever encountered before…'

And at that moment a predator flew straight onto Jem's shoulders and bore her to the ground. She landed with a thud in the dust and immediately kicked out, trying to dislodge the creature, but it had too good a grip, and too many limbs with which to maintain it.

Hobbo made a grab for the insect but couldn't get hold of it. Jem was rolling frantically from side to side, twisting and turning as the predator's curved mandibles snapped repeatedly at her throat.

'I can't get it off!' Hobbo yelled.

'It'll kill her!' shouted Mitch.

The predator's segmented body arched as it strengthened its grip and mauled Jem's head and neck. The Doctor rammed his sonic screwdriver into a gap in the creature's chitin and fired off a series of ultrasonic pulses into the soft flesh beneath. The insect let out a sudden squeal, spraying pus-like saliva from its flaying mandibles. The Doctor kept the screwdriver jammed in the carapace and activated. Slowly the beast began to let go of Jem, reluctantly tearing one leg away at a time in an effort to reach back using its many joints and remove the irritation. Teeth gritted, the Doctor increased the frequency on the screwdriver's output and suddenly many more legs were flailing madly, loosening their grip.

With a grunt of effort, Hobbo tore the thing off Jem and threw it onto the ground, where Mitch stamped his foot down on its exposed thorax, just above the point where its legs joined the body. The creature hissed and squealed and whipped its legs around but it was firmly pinned to the floor.

The Doctor pulled Jem to her feet. 'Are you all right?'

'I-I think so.' She was shaking, and there was blood on her neck where the insect's mandibles had sliced the skin.

'Cuts and contusions only,' said the Doctor briskly. 'You'll be fine!'

Hobbo bent down, gripped the sides of the insect's thrashing head and twisted. The muscles knotted in her forearms as the creature squirmed madly under Mitch's boot. Suddenly, with a loud popping crack, the head came free, gushing yellow slime and trailing long, tendon-like organs. With a snarl Hobbo threw the head away. It bounced against a wall and then rolled away, snapping and chomping at nothing before finally becoming still.

Mitch took his foot off the carcass. The legs had stopped thrashing and were slowly curling inwards, trembling as the last, autonomic impulses fired through the nervous system.

'There's more of them,' said Jem.

The insects were crawling out of the mist towards them – many more. They were climbing over the walls and down the gantries, appearing everywhere. Hundreds of them.

'Run,' said the Doctor, grabbing Jem's hand. Mitch and Hobbo sprinted after them, heading deeper into the ruins, but the horde of insects was closing in too fast, scrambling over every obstacle as they converged, and Mitch let out a sharp cry of pain as two of them leapt onto his back and took him down.

'Mitch!' Hobbo skidded to halt and turned back, a look of horror on her face as she saw the old man disappear under a river of insects. His baseball cap had landed at her feet. '*Mitch!*'

Hobbo started forward to help, but the Doctor grabbed her and held her fast. 'It's too late,' he said savagely.

The insects piled onto Mitch, mandibles snapping and ripping at him. He struggled madly beneath them, and Hobbo caught one single glimpse of his blood-streaked face looking up at her. His eyes were imploring.

'*Run!*' Mitch screamed, and then convulsed as long, piercing spikes extended from his attackers' throats and thrust deep into his body. A blood frenzy overtook the horde as they surrounded their prey, long feeding tubes protruding from between slavering mandibles to seek out the meat.

The insects lost all interest in Hobbo, Jem and the Doctor as they concentrated on the feast.

'Don't look,' the Doctor said, turning Hobbo's tear-stained face gently away. 'Just don't look.'

Chapter

15

Clara felt like she'd walked for miles. Her hair was lank with the humidity, and her clothes were soaked in sweat. 'Are you sure this is the right direction?'

Tibby stopped and looked skyward. A dim green light could be seen through the forest canopy. 'Well, if that really is the neutron star this world orbits... then yes, this is *probably* the right way.'

'It's the way we were heading in the ice age,' Balfour confirmed as he joined them. He checked his wrist panel and then looked up. His blond hair was matted against his head and his throat was shiny with sweat. The jungle cast a strange, green pallor on his skin.

'What's the hold-up?' asked Marco. He trudged into view, wiped the sleeve of his spacesuit across his face and then spat into the undergrowth.

'Just trying to get our bearings,' Clara told him.

'We could be going round in circles,' he said. 'Besides, I still don't understand where we're supposed to be headed.'

'We're trying to find the others,' Balfour reminded him patiently.

'They're probably dead.'

Clara glared at him. 'We don't know that. Until we do, we'll continue the search.'

'You're welcome to stay here if you like,' said Balfour.

Marco sniffed. 'We'd best stay together.'

Clara turned and pressed on. Her feet were heavy, and everything was becoming an effort. She couldn't even be bothered arguing with Marco. Her mouth felt dry and with a groan she realised the last time she'd had anything to drink was the Doctor's hot chocolate on board the *Alexandria*. Her stomach rumbled at the memory.

Marco continued to complain about everything: the humidity, the plants, the insects, even the direction they were going in.

'Put it this way...' said Balfour, stopping for a breather as they crossed a wide chasm bridged by a fallen tree. 'We can all carry on in this direction, or you can go back the way we came. Alone.'

Marco nodded. 'OK, we carry on.'

The chasm they were crossing disappeared into a green mist far below. The sides were carpeted in a thick, spongy moss. They walked carefully across the tree-bridge, all too aware that the bark was covered with slippery trails of white sap leaking down around the circumference and dripping into the gorge below. This leakage was caused by a number of large insects the size of cricket stumps, embedded in the bark like needles in a pin-cushion, guzzling the juice of the tree. Occasionally one of the stump-insects would quiver like an arrow striking home and then a thin stream of sap – or something – would jet out of its rear end, arcing through the air and disappearing in a rain of droplets far below.

They kept stopping to check the position of the sun. The bright spot in the sky – if that's what it was – could barely be seen through the roof of leaves and crisscrossing branches. Clara didn't really know what a non-revolving neutron star was, but it didn't shed much light, even this far back in the planet's history. The jungle was kept in perpetual gloom.

A little further on and they came to another halt. Clara was hot and dizzy now, and she guessed the others felt the same. Balfour bent over, resting his hands on his knees, unable to stand up straight any longer. Marco was panting hard and looked to be in some pain, but even he was too exhausted to complain.

'What's the hold-up?' asked Balfour eventually.

'Look ahead,' said Clara.

In front of them was another clearing, carpeted with a thick layer of matted reeds in which there were innumerable dips filled with water, or what looked like water. Growing in profusion around the water ditches were some familiar mustard-coloured plants. Each one was filled to the brim of its petal cup with thick, black spawn.

The four of them stood and stared for a full minute, each remembering the agonising death of Tanya Flexx in their own way.

'I'm not going anywhere near them,' said Tibby. She spoke very quietly, as if scared to disturb the plants.

'Me neither,' said Clara. 'But I can't see how far the plants extend. There's plenty here in the clearing – but they're also growing over there, into the jungle.'

'We could split up,' suggested Marco. 'Go around either side.'

'A minute ago you said we should stick together,' noted Balfour.

Marco sighed. 'Not now. If we go in pairs we can quickly find out which is the right way to go. I don't know about you lot, but I'm exhausted and I don't want to waste any more energy than I have to.'

Balfour turned to Clara. 'What do you think?'

'What does it matter what she thinks?' asked Marco querulously. 'Who put her in charge?'

'Who put *you* in charge?' Balfour shot back at Marco.

'Let's not argue,' said Tibby. 'It's probably a good idea. We could scout out the jungle on either side of the plants. I just want to get away from here.'

'Then it's settled,' Marco said. 'I'll go this way with Tibby. You and Clara go that way.'

He started to move off, but Clara saw the look of trepidation on Tibby's face and said, 'Wait. On second thoughts, Marco, maybe it would be best if you went with Balfour. I'll go with Tibby.'

'I'm not going with Balfour,' Marco said.

'Why not?' Balfour said.

'Well, no offence, Balfour, but you're not much use, are you? You're not qualified to do anything. You're just a spoilt rich kid who wanted an adventure. Well, you've got one – but I don't want to share it with you.'

Balfour straightened up. 'All right. Come to think of it, Marco, I don't really want to go with you, either. In fact, I can't think why I ever asked you to come on this mission in the first place.'

'You asked me to come because I was the only person with any real idea where the *Carthage* disappeared,' Marco responded. 'And therefore the only person who could help find your precious wormhole. And look where that got us.'

'Everyone can make a mistake, I suppose,' shrugged Balfour. 'You may be a pretty good archaeologist but you're a wheedling, bad-minded little fool as well.'

'OK, that's enough,' Clara said sharply. 'This isn't the school playground and it's no time to be arguing. Grow up, the pair of you. We'll split up – Balfour, you go with Tibby. I'll go with Marco.'

'But…' Marco began.

'No buts,' Clara snapped. 'Just do as you're told.'

She turned and walked off into the jungle, knowing he would follow. She knew his type only too well from Coal Hill. After a few seconds she heard him stomping through the undergrowth behind her, muttering under his breath.

Balfour turned and held out his hand to Tibby. He was standing on top of a gnarly tree trunk that had split and fallen across the path they had chosen. Tibby looked up at him, wiped the sleeve of her spacesuit across her forehead, and smiled. 'You think I need a hand?'

Balfour hesitated. 'Uh… no. Yes. I don't know. It seemed like the right thing to do.'

She took the hand and jumped up onto the tree trunk. 'Don't sweat it. We all need a hand sometimes.'

'I used to rely on Trugg all the time. He did everything

for me. Now I'm on my own… and though I miss Trugg, I do sort of like it.'

'You're not on your own, though. I'm here too.' Tibby held his gaze for just a moment. 'And so are the others. We're all in this together.'

'Hmm. Some are more in it than others. Marco doesn't strike me as much of a team player.'

'He's not,' Tibby agreed. 'But he's scared out of his wits.'

'We're all scared. There's no need to be so obnoxious about it, though.'

'True. I'm glad I'm with you, and not him.'

Balfour raised an eyebrow. 'In that case, call me Ray. I'm sick of being called Balfour. I did ask everyone at the start to call me Ray, but no one did. No one ever does.'

Tibby smiled. 'Maybe it's because you don't look like a "Ray".'

'Please tell me I look like a Ray more than I look like a "Rueun",' he laughed.

They shared the moment, and then Tibby squeezed his hand. 'Come on, then, *Ray*. Lead on.'

'I hope you've cooled off a bit,' Clara told Marco after a short while.

'Just because you're the Doctor's assistant doesn't mean you're in charge,' Marco grumbled.

'I'm not the Doctor's assistant, I'm his friend – something you wouldn't know much about.'

'Whatever. The fact is, you and the Doctor know something about this planet that you're not telling any of the others.'

Clara hesitated. 'Don't be ridiculous.'

'The others are too stupid to see it, but I'm not,' Marco went on. 'You're after something here, and you're trying to keep it to yourselves.'

He'd drawn level with Clara now as they walked. There was a sly tone in his voice that Clara really didn't like. 'You don't know what you're talking about.'

'Don't I?' Marco smirked. 'I've met people like you and the Doctor before: freeloaders, tagging along with archaeological expeditions in the hope of discovering some treasure and sharing in it.'

'You're wrong.'

'Am I? What about the Glamour?'

This stopped Clara in her tracks. She turned to look at him, feeling the sweat turn cold all over her body. 'What do you know about the Glamour?'

'Not much. Only what I overheard you and the Doctor saying. Don't look so shocked, Clara. The *Alexandria* wasn't that big a ship. You didn't think you and the Doctor could keep your little secrets and whispers to yourselves, did you? I heard your little chat in the cabin. I don't fully understand what the Glamour is but I'm pretty certain it's valuable – otherwise you and the Doctor wouldn't have risked your lives to come to this benighted place.'

Clara recalled the moment when the *Alexandria* had first run into trouble. She and the Doctor had rushed out of her cabin and straight into Marco. He must have been listening outside. 'You don't know anything about it,' she said uncertainly.

'So tell me. Maybe I could share in the bounty.'

'Get lost.'

Clara turned and walked on, striding purposefully into the jungle, her heart thumping and her mind racing. Where *was* the Doctor? What was she going to do without him?

They continued in silence for a while, skirting around the area where the mustard-coloured plants were. Every time Clara saw one of the things poking through the undergrowth, she cut a little more to the left to avoid them. She made sure she kept the pace up, just to avoid giving Marco the opportunity to talk. She could hear him panting behind her, every breath taken by the humid air. They were forced to halt when they reached a near-vertical wall of foliage. It rose up sharply from the undergrowth to a height of around four metres, where it ended in an unnaturally level edge.

'What's this?' Clara wondered, following the wall.

'Looks like the jungle has grown over something solid,' Marco said, following her.

They found a cut in the wall and climbed through it, and then up a series of long moss-covered steps.

'They're ruins,' realised Clara. 'Something was built here…'

'They must have been here for an age,' Marco said. There were mounds and angular banks of jungle, threaded with roots and vines, but clearly discernible, like a building had been grown out of the abundant plant life. 'It would take hundreds and thousands of years for the jungle to reclaim it like this.'

Clara reached the top of one level and looked out at a

long avenue of trees sprouting from angular blocks. 'It's like a city,' she panted. 'Buried in the forest.'

'Hey, look down there,' Marco said, peering over the edge of the rise.

Below them was a forest of the mustard plants, each of them full of black spawn. Some of them were quietly bubbling, and the petals of the flowers were flexing gently, getting ready, it seemed, to close up and squirt out their horrid contents at the least provocation. Clara felt nauseous just looking at them.

Suddenly Clara was grabbed from behind and shoved towards the edge. She would have gone clean over if instinct hadn't made her stiffen up and dig her heels hard into the ground. Her forward motion interrupted, Marco had to struggle with her but then lost his own footing and Clara pushed herself violently backwards. Marco sprang to his feet, his face twisted into an angry snarl. He grabbed Clara again as she stood up, trying to force her back to the edge. It had become a physical battle now. Marco was bigger and heavier, and there was no avoiding the fact that Clara was going to go over. She resolved there and then to take him with her. She grabbed the collar of his spacesuit and yanked him towards her, using his own momentum against him. They fell together and her head jerked back as she landed with her shoulders over the edge of the precipice. Marco was on top of her. His teeth were bared, his eyes blazing with murder. Clara tried to remember what Danny had once told her about basic self-defence but her mind had blanked. There was only the survival instinct operating now. Somehow she jerked her knee up and Marco yelped furiously, loosening his grip. Clara tore herself free, rolled, scrambling on hands and knees, pulling herself along the grass away from the mustard plants.

Marco stood up behind her, just as Balfour and Tibby burst through the trees. Balfour immediately helped Clara to her feet.

'He's trying to kill me!' Clara choked.

'Rubbish,' Marco said. 'The stupid girl nearly walked right over the edge. I had to grab her to save her and we fell.'

'Liar!'

Marco took a deep breath, hands on hips. 'She's been hysterical ever since.'

'Don't let him anywhere near me,' warned Clara.

'It's all right,' Balfour said. 'Tibby and I are here now. Nothing's going to happen.'

'Nothing did happen,' Marco said.

'What made you come back?' Clara asked Balfour.

'We didn't. We circled right around the spawn plants and then Tibby heard the commotion.'

'What are these ruins?' Tibby asked. 'An ancient city?'

'Must be,' said Marco, looking thoughtful. 'Perhaps we aren't the first visitors to this world after all.'

'We're definitely not the only ones here now,' said Tibby, pointing past Marco, towards the depths of jungle beyond. 'Look,' she said.

Drifting through the darkness between the trees were a number of blue, glowing figures. The wraiths emerged from the square edge of the forest, shimmering like moonbeams, tall, hooded, not of this world. Or any world, perhaps.

'The ghosts!' gasped Marco. 'They've followed us from the ice age! What do they want?'

He backed away from the wraiths until he was standing behind Balfour and Clara, and then the jungle around them began to blur, as if a giant and invisible hand had swept across a still-wet painting of reality.

'Time flux,' Clara said, the words clogging in her mouth as the jungle started to recede, and everything around her seemed to fall away, dragging her with it into complete darkness.

Chapter

16

The skin of Jem's face and neck was covered with bruises and lacerations. Hobbo tore off some material from her jacket and folded it into a wad of cloth that could be used to staunch the bleeding.

'I'm sorry about Mitch,' Jem said quietly.

'Yeah,' Hobbo replied. Her voice was dull, distant. Mechanically, she checked the wounds again and reapplied the dressing as best she could.

'It all happened so fast,' Jem said.

'Yeah.'

'I… I know what it feels like.'

Hobbo focused on her properly for the first time. Her face looked stiff, awkward, as if it wasn't really hers, or she wasn't in full control of the way it looked. 'Yeah. I reckon you do.'

They'd left the insects to their abominable feast and moved away from the area, walking quickly and, it seemed at times, aimlessly through the ruins. Eventually they had found a secluded area and stopped to rest. They were lost, tired and hungry, and Hobbo was very quiet and withdrawn, but at least there were no insects around here.

The Doctor scanned Jem with the sonic screwdriver. 'No sign of any toxins, thank goodness.'

They helped Jem to her feet, Hobbo keeping the cloth against the worst of her cuts. It was already stippled with red blotches.

A blue glow appeared in a gap in the nearest wall, and a group of wraiths floated through it, tall and hooded.

'I'm beginning to hate the sight of those guys,' Hobbo said.

'The Phaeron,' said the Doctor, almost mesmerised by the sight. 'Beings of pure dark matter…'

'Can they see us?'

'Ask Jem.'

'I think they can,' said Jem, holding out a hand towards the glimmering apparitions.

The hooded figures reached out towards her, mimicking the gesture… and then faded from view, until all that was left was the swirling grey fog.

'Remarkable!' said the Doctor.

'How'd she do that?' asked Hobbo.

'I'm not sure,' said the Doctor. 'But Jem can sense the way dark matter interacts with the universe. Maybe that's how the Phaeron communicate too.'

'But is that even possible?' asked Jem.

'It must be. The language difference could be a problem – but if the Phaeron were as powerful and advanced as I'm beginning to suspect they were, then I'm sure they'll find a way around that.'

'You keep talkin' about them in the past one minute

an' then in the here and now,' Hobbo said. 'Are these guys history or not?'

'Past, present, future – none of these things mean anything to the Phaeron. They exist beyond space and time now.'

'How can that be?'

'No idea!' The Doctor's eyes had taken on a manically curious gleam. 'But I intend to find out.'

The darkness was not absolute. There was a faint luminescence coming from the lichen which clung to the walls. Tibby Vent sat shivering in the void, trying not to make any noise, urging her vision to adjust to the utter gloom. It was cold in here, after the heat of the jungle. She was definitely inside something; when she moved, her boots made scuffing noises on some kind of hard, flat surface like concrete or metal and the noises echoed.

There was a smell, too. Dampness; not the humidity of the forest but the cold condensation of a deep cave or basement. When she touched the floor, she could feel spores of lichen, and trace thin, stringy weeds and crumbling flakes of dirt.

After a long while she thought she could see someone else in the dark – lying down, asleep or otherwise unconscious. They weren't dead because she could hear them breathing. Minutes passed and she did not move, dared not move, but she strained her eyes until she picked out the shape of a spacesuit and the long, dark hair of Clara Oswald.

Slowly, cautiously, Tibby unfolded her legs and crawled

across the floor to where Clara lay. She touched her, but there was no response. She was out cold. There was someone else next to her – Ray Balfour. She felt a flood of relief. He lay on his back, arms out, mouth open. He was on the verge of snoring as the breath caught on his slack, unconscious throat.

The terrors of the last few hours had started to dig into Tibby's nerves. She could feel her pulse racing, her breath hurrying. She wasn't far from panic. She couldn't stay here much longer. She felt alone and vulnerable and lost.

A face loomed before her, visible only as a grey mask in the faint light. It was Marco Spritt and Tibby let out a gasp of shock.

'I didn't know you were there!' she said. 'Why didn't you say something? I've been scared witless!'

Marco spoke in a whisper. 'I don't know what kind of a man you think I am, Tibby, but it's not me you need protection from.'

'Why? What else is there? Where are we?'

He held a finger against her lips. 'Shh. Quietly. One thing at a time. I've seen more of those blue ghost things floating around here. Let's not attract their attention.'

Tibby bit her lip. 'We need to wake up Clara and Ray.'

'Who?

'Ray. Balfour.' Tibby met Marco's stare. 'We need to wake him up, and Clara.'

'No.' Marco was emphatic about that. 'They're out cold. We have to move.'

'We can't just leave them!'

'We'll have to if we're going to get help.' Marco stood

up and, gripping Tibby by the arm, pulled her to her feet with him.

'Help?' Hope flickered into life inside Tibby's chest.

'You don't think I'd just leave them here, do you?'

'Do you know where we are?'

'Yes.' Marco smiled in the darkness. 'I know where we are.'

The Doctor, Hobbo and Jem were making their way deeper into the ruins. They were following a trio of Phaeron wraiths as they floated, seemingly in and out of reality, ahead of them.

'Where are they takin' us?' asked Hobbo quietly.

'Who says they're taking us anywhere?' replied the Doctor. 'We're just following them. They seem to know where they're going, after all.'

'What if they just disappear? We can't follow them into nowhere.'

The three wraiths faded from view as she spoke, the faint nimbus of blue light evaporating into the gloom behind them.

'We're close,' said Jem.

'Close to what?' asked the Doctor.

'The Imperfection.'

Rising out of the rusted crags, shrouded in coils of thick grey mist, was a large obelisk with a wide, rectangular opening. Huge fungoid growths were sprouting from the patches of lichen clinging to the rusted metal surface, and hanging down over the darkened passage like a thin curtain of weeds.

'Is that it?' Hobbo wondered.

'I don't think so,' said the Doctor. 'It looks more like an entrance of some kind.' He pushed aside some of the dangling weeds and wrinkled his nose.

'I don't like it the look of it,' Hobbo said. 'And it stinks.'

'Cyanobacteria living in the fungus,' explained the Doctor. 'The corrosion and the damp allow for algal cells to develop. They're tiny, harmless composite organisms that can sprout up anywhere if the conditions are right.'

'I don't mean that.' Hobbo circled the obelisk, examining it in some detail. 'I just don't like the *look* of it. Something about it doesn't feel right. Like it's strange, and familiar, all at the same time.'

'Could it be something to do with the Phaeron?' wondered Jem. 'You said they existed beyond time and space. That might account for any sense of déjà vu.'

'It's possible,' said the Doctor thoughtfully.

'Wait, look,' said Hobbo, pointing at the entrance to the obelisk. 'They're back…'

There was a distinct, azure glow developing in the shadows, and a number of ghostly forms began to manifest. They grew ever more apparent, and more detailed, until three hooded figures stood in the darkness, staring out at the Doctor, Jem and Hobbo.

The Doctor stared back at them. The faces inside the hoods were mostly concealed, but in the nearest he could make out a long, disjointed proboscis surmounted by a pair of deeply set eyes the colour of blood. He was strongly reminded of the appearance of plague doctors during the eighteenth century on Earth, who wore beak-like masks stuffed with herbs and salts to prevent the wearer breathing in any kind of airborne communicable disease. There was a distinctly insectoid appearance to the long, pointed faces too; perhaps, considered the Doctor, the proboscis had its origins as some kind of organ for feeding or sucking. It wasn't an altogether pleasant thought, when matched with the blank, unmoving eyes.

'What do they want?' asked Hobbo warily.

'They want us to go in,' said Jem.

The Doctor turned to the astrogator. 'Can you communicate with them directly?'

'No,' Jem replied. 'But I can sense what they want... what they require.'

'And they require us to go inside?'

'They want the Imperfection.'

'Do they, indeed?' The Doctor thought about this for a moment and then turned back to the obelisk. The figures had disappeared.

'We should go in,' said Jem, starting forward.

'Wait a sec,' Hobbo interrupted, stopping her. 'What if we're the "imperfection" they want? What if it's all some kinda trap?'

'It isn't,' said Jem simply.

The Doctor walked forward, hesitated at the fronds of weed that hung from the mantel, and then stepped through. He turned around and looked out of the obelisk at Hobbo and Jem, his eyes invisible in the shadows. 'I think I'm beginning to understand,' he said. 'Come on, slowcoaches.' And with that he took a step backwards and disappeared into the darkness completely.

*

Marco was pulling Tibby along the passageway. 'Keep up,' he urged.

'Where are we going?'

'You'll see.'

A blue light appeared at the end of the passage and Marco yanked Tibby back, pushing her against the wall. She felt the coldness and held her breath as one of the tall, robed figures materialised in the darkness. Its hood moved as whatever lay within began to turn towards them. A pair of dark eyes peered chillingly from a long, aquiline face and then the vision was gone. The blue light faded and darkness swept back into its place.

Tibby breathed again. 'I think we should go back for Clara and Ray.'

'There isn't time!' snapped Marco. 'Those ghosts are everywhere. We have to find the others first; *then* we can help Clara and Balfour.'

He tried to pull her after him, but she refused to move. 'I don't like this. I don't know where we are or where we're going.'

'Relax. I do.'

'So where are the others?'

'I'll show you.' Marco adopted a reasonable tone. 'Look, you want to see the Doctor again, don't you?'

More hope surging through her, an instinctive response to something she had dared not to think about for so long now. 'The Doctor's here? Have you seen him?'

'Of course he's here. And all the others, no doubt.'

'How do you know? Have you seen them?'

'Listen, Tibby. We can either stand here doing a full

question and answer session or we can get on with it. Trust me – I know where we are now and where we need to go. Now come on!'

Marco grabbed her hand – better than her arm, at least – and led the way further into the darkness.

'What the hell *was* this place?' Hobbo wondered aloud, her voice echoing backwards and forwards along the tunnel.

The Doctor either didn't hear her or didn't bother to reply. He strode confidently ahead, using his sonic screwdriver to light the way. The cool green glow revealed what seemed to be an intricate cave system carved out by unknown hands. The circular walls and floor were oddly smooth and etched with obscure markings.

Hobbo hurried to keep up. 'This is gettin' weirder all the time. Do you know where we're even goin'?'

'I'm trying to home in on the signal from my TARDIS.' The Doctor paused to fiddle with the screwdriver for a minute and then held it up to his ear, listening carefully. 'It's getting weaker all the time, even though we seem to be getting closer. I don't understand…'

'This place is like a maze,' said Jem.

A blue glow appeared around the corner, and the now familiar robed shape stepped into view. Jem watched in barely concealed awe as the birdlike face turned slowly within the shadow of its hood to look directly at her. Nictitating eyelids flicked across the dark eyes and then the wraith vanished.

'We must keep on,' Jem said. 'Go deeper into the caves. The Phaeron are waiting for us. They're calling us!'

'Not that way,' said the Doctor, sweeping his sonic around in a circle. 'This way... the TARDIS is this way.'

'But the Phaeron are waiting, Doctor!'

'Let 'em wait!' The Doctor shrugged. 'They've been waiting here for a billion years. They exist beyond time and space, remember. They can wait a little longer.'

'Hold on.' Hobbo called them over to where she had reached to touch the nearest wall. 'Look at this.'

They were standing in circular passageway with alcoves spaced at regular intervals. The light from the Doctor's sonic screwdriver picked out more markings; regular, square indentations and circles. Hobbo pointed to the markings on the floor, scuffing away the dust and dirt with her boot to reveal a diamond pattern.

'What is it?' Jem asked.

'I'm not sure,' Hobbo said. 'They remind me of somethin', though.'

'C'mon!' admonished the Doctor, as if he was amazed that neither of them had spotted something that was glaringly obvious. 'Don't tell me you can't see it?'

Hobbo scratched her head and looked puzzled. 'It sure looks familiar. I dunno why 'cos I ain't *ever* been here before. I can swear to that.'

'I know you've never been here before,' the Doctor said. 'None of us have. But you've been somewhere very similar.'

Hobbo looked around her, mouth hanging open as realisation dawned. 'You *knew*?'

'I thought it was obvious!' he said, perplexed.

'When did you know?'

'As soon as we saw the obelisk. It was the only thing that made sense.'

'Well I'm not sure about makin' any sense,' said Hobbo. 'But you're damn right, I shoulda seen it already. I only wish Mitch was here to see it too.'

'See what?' asked Jem.

'This whole ruin,' explained the Doctor, 'is not the ruin of an ancient building. It is the ruin of an ancient spacecraft.'

'The passageways, the corridors…' said Hobbo. 'The obelisk. I knew I recognised the markings on the wall! They were sub-control panels and data ports. It was an auxiliary airlock – or the remains of one at least.'

'Calcified and covered in lichen and grime and the solidified dust and dirt of millennia,' the Doctor agreed. 'Barely recognisable – unless you've spent your whole life in spaceships.'

Hobbo wiped at the surface of one wall, scraping away at the dirt. Bits crumbled and fell into dust, revealing something shiny and metallic beneath.

'Allow me,' said the Doctor, brandishing the sonic screwdriver again. He pointed it at the wall and the tip glowed bright green. The rough surface cracked and then flaked away, resonated into dust by the sonic pulses. More metal was revealed, reflecting the green light brightly. 'This isn't just any spaceship, either,' he said. He swept the beam of the screwdriver along the wall, and a huge section of it crumbled way, clattering to the floor to reveal a large, engraved plaque which read, simply:

CARTHAGE

Chapter

17

'The *Carthage*!' Hobbo touched the inscription as if she needed physical confirmation that it was actually there. More grime fell away under her touch to reveal a series of rusted ideograms.

'This is the ship Marco was looking for,' said Jem. 'The one captained by his mother.'

'It has aged millions of years but the basic structure is still intact,' said the Doctor. He pointed at the ideograms. 'We're now standing in what was the connecting corridor to the data core.'

'But how did the *Carthage* end up here?' Hobbo asked. 'Like this?'

'It never made it to the Andromeda galaxy at all. It must have broken out of the wormhole and crashed on this planet, just like the *Alexandria*.'

'So it's been sitting here for millennia, caught in the time fields,' realised Jem sadly. 'Just crumbling away…'

'If this is the mid-level access corridor,' said the Doctor, thinking aloud, 'then the data core will be right around the corner. Hobbo, do you think it could still be intact?'

'These old ships had slow-decay astronic power cells threaded right the way through the superstructure. Cheap an' cheerful – but above all, long-lastin'. It ain't impossible.'

'What have you got in mind?' wondered Jem as they worked their away further along the corridor.

'He's thinkin' about accessing the ship's computer memory banks,' Hobbo realised. 'Check the flight recorder – find out exactly what happened to the crew of seventy-seven. Isn't that right, Doc?'

'Among other things, yes.'

They turned the corner and passed through a broken, rectangular hole in the wall that might have once been a subsidiary airlock. On the other side was a tall, circular chamber, its high walls overgrown with dank, fibrous weeds and cobwebs. The Doctor used his sonic screwdriver to illuminate the area, the bright green light sending thin-legged spiders hurrying for the shadows.

Lying on the floor in the middle of the room was Clara Oswald.

'Typical,' said the Doctor. 'We're busy making the discovery of the century and Clara's snoring on the floor.' He poked her with the toe of his boot. 'Oi, come on, sleepyhead. Up you get.'

'What's she doin' here?' Hobbo asked. She began to search the darker corners of the room. 'Where are the others? Where's Balfour?'

Clara groaned and Jem helped her to sit up. 'It's OK, Clara. We're here. You're safe.'

Clara squinted up into a brilliant emerald light as the

Doctor scanned her with the sonic screwdriver. 'I know this is *such* a cliché – but where am I?'

'You're on board the *Carthage*,' said the Doctor. 'You've missed everything. Now get up, there's nothing wrong with you apart from the usual.'

'The usual?' Clara winced as Jem and Hobbo helped her to her feet.

'Well you can't expect miracles at your age, Clara.'

'How are you feeling?' Jem asked.

'Cold and aching, but otherwise OK, thanks.'

'That's the spirit,' nodded the Doctor. 'Never mind the years, just keep battling on.'

Clara looked around with sudden, hollow-eyed urgency. 'Where are the others? Where's Tibby?'

'We don't know. We've just found you here alone. Have you seen Balfour? Or Tanya and Marco?' asked Jem.

Clara closed her eyes on a painful memory. 'Tanya's dead. She was… killed in the jungle.'

'Jungle?'

'Long story. There was a time flux – two of them. We all ended up here after the last one. We were all together when we got here, I'm sure of it, but I passed out…' Clara rubbed at her eyes. 'I don't know why, I'm sorry. I'm not usually the fainting kind.'

'It's OK,' Jem said gently. 'We've all been through a lot. We lost Mitch.'

'Oh no.' Clara looked to the Doctor, who simply nodded sadly and shook his head. Clara turned to look at Hobbo, who was still pacing around the room, checking the wall panels, scratching the dirt away from one section after another. Losing Mitch, however it happened, must have hit Hobbo hardest. It looked as though she was keeping herself busy in order not to think about it.

'Balfour and Tibby were with me when the last time flux occurred, I'm sure of it,' Clara said. 'And Marco too. He tried to kill me in the jungle.'

'Kill you?'

'He tried to throw me into some plants that spat a kind of goo. The same plants that killed Tanya. It was horrible.'

'Then where is Marco now?' asked Hobbo.

The Doctor's frown intensified dangerously. 'We're on the *Carthage*. There's only one place he'll go.'

Marco dragged Tibby down a long corridor into a hallway with steep, sloping walls. They climbed through a narrow gap where a heavy sliding door had got stuck halfway about a million years previously and was now rusted and cultivating a thick layer of mould. The floor crunched beneath their boots as they moved. Tibby guessed generations of rats had lived and bred and mutated and died here, leaving behind a carpet of hardened dung and tiny, misshapen bones.

'What is this place?' she asked.

'This is the stasis deck,' he said. He walked slowly along one side of the hallway, examining the walls that sloped up and away from him at forty-five degrees. Every so often there was a recess or cutting in the wall, full of matted vegetation and crawling things.

'You knew exactly how to get here, didn't you?'

'Once I realised where I was, yes. I've made a study of

the *Carthage*, remember. I've pored over the specifications and history. I know every centimetre of this ship.' Marco stopped at one section of the wall and squatted to examine the base. He pulled away a web of thin, dry roots that had grown with infinite patience in the dark, tracing the edge of the floor and rising like slow, explorative, fingers up the wall. He yanked them aside and brushed at the dirt beneath. Metal shone dully.

'The *Carthage* had stasis tanks for every crewmember,' he explained. 'It was a deep-space exploration vessel, and sometimes the crew would go into hypersleep for the longer voyages between the most distant stars.'

Tibby shivered. The hallway was long. If this was where the stasis chambers were, surely the crew couldn't still be in them?

'The *Carthage* has decayed and aged,' said Marco, 'but there's still low-level power in some of the basic operating systems.'

'How do you know?'

He looked up at her with a scornful expression. 'Hello? Look around you! See anything?'

Tibby could see the other stasis tanks, leaning back in the walls, row after room. 'Just the tanks.'

'But you can *see* them. So: light.'

With a start Tibby realised that he was correct. Along the ceiling and top edge of the walls were softly illuminated panels, barely noticeable except for the faint, even light they shed. It was a dirty, yellow light, but they were working nonetheless.

Marco scraped at the surface of the tank. 'The *Carthage*

was built to last. The stasis tanks should still be functional, doing what they were designed to do – keep the crew alive.'

'But they must be ancient now,' Tibby said. 'They can't be working after all this time, surely?'

'Why not?' Marco frowned at the thought. 'Look.' He pointed to the section of the deck where he'd been working. At the base was a metal panel, pitted and rusted, but with one slowly blinking light now revealed. 'Minimal power but enough to maintain the stasis field inside the unit.'

'This is a particular unit, isn't it?' Tibby was staring at the metal panel. There was a screen built into it, misty and dull, but there were some digital figures still visible:

Caitlin Spritt, Capt. 77389-89

'You shouldn't do this,' Tibby said quietly. 'You really shouldn't, Marco.'

He glared at her, his eyes full of determination. 'Why not? This is what I came for. What I joined the *Alexandria* mission for! I've found the *Carthage*, Tibby. And now I've found *her*.'

Marco traced the edge of the stasis tank with the tips of his fingers, almost lovingly, perhaps reverently. 'Captain Spritt,' he breathed. 'It's time to wake up.'

He thumbed a sequence of controls on the base panel and lights flickered on all around the unit, stretching right up into the wall. Similar lights began to flicker on all the units, creating a strobing illumination along the hallway.

As Tibby watched, she saw Hobbo and Clara come running through the airlock and felt a huge rush of relief.

'Tibby!' cried Clara, rushing forward. Behind her came the Doctor and Jem.

Marco stood up and pulled a small, tubular device from his spacesuit pocket. He pointed it at Hobbo as she approached and the engineer pulled up warily. 'Whoa. That's an ion bonder, and it ain't yours, pal.'

'I know. I found it in the engineering section on the *Alexandria*. You should have been more careful with your tools.' Marco kept the ion bonder trained on Mitch, but in the relatively narrow confines of the stasis hallway he could cover all the others.

'What's an ion bonder?' asked Clara.

'Fixin' tool,' said Hobbo. 'Not much of a weapon, but enough at close range.'

The Doctor stepped forward, his face drawn and sombre. 'I hope you're not planning to activate any of these stasis tanks, Marco, because that would be a horrible mistake.'

'It's too late,' Marco replied. More lights were flickering on along the hallway, and a low, steady hum could be heard.

'I always knew you were an idiot, Marco,' said the Doctor. 'But this is taking idiocy to a completely new level. You don't know what you're doing.'

'I know exactly what I'm doing,' Marco snapped. Spittle gathered at the corner of his mouth. He pointed the ion bonder at the Doctor's chest. 'Take another step towards me and you get it.'

'Oh, I get it, all right,' nodded the Doctor. 'Poor little Marco's come looking for his mummy. Well, Marco…' The Doctor pointed at the stasis tank. 'Is this your mummy?'

The tank had lit up from within. A chime sounded as the machinery inside reached its optimal level. A long metal screen slid back, up into the slope of the wall, shedding dust and grime and lichen as it disappeared into a narrow slot. Beneath it was a transparent lid, and under that could be seen a prone figure. It wasn't clearly visible because the plasteel window had clouded with age.

Marco glanced down at the tank nearest to him, and then quickly looked back at the others. He kept the ion bonder level, his finger shaking on the activator. 'Don't come any closer!'

'I don't want to, believe me,' said the Doctor. He regarded Marco with baleful, hooded eyes. 'In fact, I'd advise you to step away yourself.'

'You're spoiling this!'

All along the hallway, more of the stasis units were illuminating, humming, the metal hatches sliding back with long, grinding noises. Inside each one was the shape of a human being.

But Marco was only interested in the tank next to him. He grabbed Tibby and pulled her tight against him, pressing the ion bonder into the side of her neck.

Hobbo, who had been moving steadily, slowly forward as the Doctor talked, froze in her tracks. 'Hey, don't be stupid, Marco. You could kill her with that.'

'Just stay where you are!' Saliva flew from Marco's lips as he kept Tibby positioned in front of him, the ion bonder jammed against her throat. His eyes turned to look down at the stasis unit as the plasteel window cracked away from its housing with a soft, pneumatic hiss and lifted on a hinge to reveal what lay within.

Tibby let out a gasp of horror. Lying inside the tank was

the dark husk of a person. The skull was covered in a thin layer of dry flesh, shrunk tight to the bone, the eye sockets nothing but withered creases. Grey hair hung, stiff and brittle, against the shoulders.

'Oh no,' Marco said, choking. 'Oh no, please no, tell me it's not true...'

'They're dead, Marco,' said Tibby. 'They're all dead.'

Every tank had opened to reveal a similar sight: a shrivelled corpse. Not one of the *Carthage* crew had survived.

'There wasn't enough power left to keep the stasis tanks goin',' said Hobbo quietly. She almost sounded sorry for Marco. Almost. 'They were never gonna last, you dumb fool.'

'It's terrible,' said Clara, holding the Doctor's arm. A fetid stench was beginning to fill the hallway and she covered her mouth.

'It's worse than that, I'm afraid,' said the Doctor. 'This entire spaceship is contained in a massively fluctuating time field. Those stasis units work on time suppression fields. The two things won't mix.'

'What'll happen?' Clara asked.

'I dread to think.'

Marco bared his teeth. 'Shut up! Stop talking, all of you!' His eyes were fixed on the cadaver in the stasis unit. The thing that had once been his mother, someone he had never even known alive. He could not look away from the grinning skull.

Hobbo wanted to move closer, but she could see the knuckles on Marco's hand were white where they gripped the ion bonder. At this range the damage to Tibby Vent would be instantly fatal. Hobbo dared not move. 'For pity's sake, Spritt,' she said. 'Get away from there.'

'No...' Marco breathed. A look of complete despair overtook his twisted features. He was still staring at the corpse in the tank. The skeletal remains within were already crumbling. A shimmering field of displaced air slowly expanded from within the tank, carrying the dust of ages with it.

'Oh no...' said Tibby.

'Doctor, what's happening?' Clara demanded.

'The temporal suppression field inside the tank is reacting with the time field outside. What that means is anyone's guess.'

Marco let out a long, low groan, reaching out to the emaciated husk in the casket. His hand closed on the flaking remains, and dust ran through his fingers.

'Stop! Stop it!' he screamed. 'Mother!'

Tibby grabbed the ion bonder and twisted it out of Marco's hand, pulling away and running to the Doctor and Clara as Marco continued to scream.

The conflicting time fields enveloped Marco and he started to change. Hair erupted from his head in a sudden, greying torrent, a beard curling out of his face, whitening and fading as the skin beneath aged and sagged.

'Time acceleration!' said the Doctor. 'We've got to get away from here!'

Marco's teeth cracked open and his jawbone, rotting at the hinge, fell away to reveal a twisted, blackened tongue. He was still screaming.

The Doctor pulled Tibby and Clara away, herding them with Hobbo and Jem back through the airlock.

The last they saw of Marco Spritt was the papery flesh splitting and falling away from his bones. He let out a final, clotted shriek of agony as the Doctor pointed his sonic screwdriver at the airlock. The tip flashed green and a shrill whine filled the corridor. Slowly, and with a terrible, metallic grinding noise, the airlock door began to move. It jerked along runners in the bulkhead, dislodging weeds and spiders, and then finally clicked home. The sounds of the stasis chamber were abruptly cut off.

Chapter

18

'What just happened?' asked Clara shakily. 'How could anyone age so quickly?'

'The time fields cancelled each other out,' the Doctor said. 'Nothing but ashes in there now.'

'That was a terrible thing for anyone to see,' said Clara. She looked sadly at Tibby. 'Are you all right?'

Tibby nodded. 'Better now that I'm out of there.'

Clara took the opportunity to pull off the rest of her spacesuit. Her work clothes were rumpled and in need of the washing machine, and the very thought of the simple, mundane chores of everyday life was both surreal and reassuring.

The Doctor was fiddling with his sonic screwdriver again, eyebrows working hard. He clicked it open and swept it around the passageway, taking a number of readings.

'What is it?' Clara asked, noticing the ever-deepening frown of worry on his face.

'I'm scanning for the TARDIS... but not picking up any signal at all now. Not even a weak one.'

Clara felt a flutter of anxiety. 'Then where is it?'

'I have no idea. I was getting so close… the signal was weak, but now there's just nothing.' His eyes were suddenly full of clouds. 'Nothing at all.'

The *Carthage* was now utterly silent. The five of them huddled together as the stillness closed in around them. 'Feels like the place is suddenly deserted,' said Clara with a shiver. Her voice echoed back and forth along the passageways.

The Doctor had taken out his key to the TARDIS and held the tip of the sonic screwdriver against the metal. The screwdriver glowed green but nothing happened to the key and he let out a hiss of annoyance.

'What was that supposed to do?'

'I thought I might be able to boost the TARDIS signal through the key,' he said. 'If the TARDIS was anywhere here or now the key would glow.'

'It's not glowing,' Clara noted.

'No, it's not.' Screwdriver and key disappeared back into his pockets and the Doctor ran his fingers backwards and forwards through his untidy grey hair. 'Come on, Doctor! Think! You're missing something, you silly old fool.'

'We're stuck here, aren't we?' said Tibby quietly.

The Doctor suddenly stood up straight, one long bony finer held up like an aerial above him. 'Question!' he said loudly. The word echoed around and around. 'What's the *Carthage* doing here?'

They all looked at him but didn't say a word.

The Doctor's eyes were like little bright sparks in the gloom, his curly hair fizzing out of the top of his head as if it could barely contain the energy inside. 'I mean, what's the *Carthage* actually *doing* here?' he repeated.

'It's not doing anything,' said Clara.

'Exactly.' The Doctor beamed. 'It's not doing anything. But it should be. It should be falling back through time like the rest of us were. There hasn't been another time flux since we all arrived here, and there's no sign of another one happening. Why?'

'I don't think any of us really know why,' said Tibby.

'Yes you do,' said the Doctor. 'You just said it yourself a second ago but I was too stupid to listen.'

'What did she say?' asked Clara.

'She said, "We're stuck here, aren't we?"' The Doctor looked at them each in turn, meeting each individual gaze. He gave Tibby Vent a wink and she smiled uncertainly. 'We're stuck. The *Carthage* is *stuck.*'

'And knowing that helps us… how?' asked Clara.

'Since we crashed on this planet we've been falling backwards in time, millions of years. Think of it like a well. We came in at the top and fell down the well. Deeper and deeper. If we look up, we can just see daylight, a tiny little disc of light no bigger than a coin. But we drop again, even further, until that little disc of light is just a dot – and then nothing. We can't even see the opening any more, we're so deep. It's dark. It's cold. We're alone.'

'Perhaps we've just reached the bottom of the well,' suggested Tibby.

'Yes, that's a good theory,' the Doctor said, 'but it doesn't fit here. Because there is no bottom to time. It just goes deeper and deeper, for ever.'

'But we're stuck?' prompted Hobbo.

'And there has to be a reason for that,' the Doctor said.

'Perhaps I can help you there, Doctor.'

It was a voice none of them expected. They all turned together to see a man standing at the end of the passageway. His hand was raised in greeting, and there was a bright, cheery smile on his tanned face.

'Balfour!'

They rushed to greet him but Balfour held up his hands. 'We've no time for all that, I'm afraid...'

'But where have you been?' demanded Tibby. 'We've been worried sick!'

'What happened?' asked Clara. 'The last time we saw you was in the jungle, just before—'

'I know,' Balfour smiled again. 'I woke up with you here. There was no sign of Tibby or Marco. You were out cold so I went to look for help. I wandered around the place for absolutely ages – but I did eventually find something that might be of use.'

There was a collective gasp of approval and relief and everyone started talking at once.

'What, exactly?' asked the Doctor, speaking louder than anybody else.

'There's a way out of here,' Balfour said. 'Back to our own time.'

'Oh thank goodness!' exclaimed Tibby.

'That's fantastic news,' said Clara.

'Come on, I'll show you!' Balfour said happily.

'Looks like we may not be stuck after all, eh, Doc?' said Hobbo.

The Doctor said nothing. He followed Clara and the others as Raymond Balfour led them further through the *Carthage*'s ancient interior.

'You won't believe it,' said Balfour as they walked. 'I didn't when I saw it. But I think you're going to be very pleased…'

He led the way up a sloping section and through a wide, rusted airlock. They followed him into a circular room not dissimilar to the flight deck on the *Alexandria*. Lights glowed dimly in the ceiling and around the walls, and on some of the instrument panels.

'Welcome to the bridge of the *Carthage!*' said Balfour, waving a hand grandly around the chamber.

'Hey, it looks like it's still in workin' order,' said Hobbo in surprise, checking some of the control panels. The metal was rusted and patched with lichen, and there were thin weeds sprouting here and there, but it wasn't beyond imagining that the ship could still fly. 'I said these things were built to last, didn't I?'

Hobbo was delighted, eagerly checking one control panel after another. Balfour beamed happily.

But Clara noticed that Jem did not look so pleased. Tibby saw it too. The astrogator, who had been quiet for a long time now, seemed close to tears.

'Jem, what's the matter?' Clara asked.

'I don't know,' she replied. She reached out a hand and held on to Clara for support. 'I… I don't feel so good. It's like I'm not properly here.'

The Doctor examined her closely, lifting her face towards his so that he could look into her eyes. 'What is it, Jem? Is it the voices? Is it the Phaeron?'

'They're coming,' Jem said.

'Who are coming?' asked Balfour. 'What's going on?'

'The deeper we fell through time, the more Jem became attuned to the Phaeron,' explained the Doctor. 'They are more advanced, and more dangerous than I ever realised. They are practically made of dark matter – and Jem's senses are telepathically attuned to dark matter.'

'The Phaeron are still alive?' Tibby said, almost breathless with excitement.

'Not in any way you or I can understand,' the Doctor said. 'They exist outside and at one with time and space. That's why we keep seeing glimpses of them – the blue wraiths – and Jem has been able to communicate with them, after a fashion. It's not perfect, but—'

'They are coming,' blurted Jem suddenly, her voice descending to a low growl. 'They are coming.'

The Doctor stared intensely at her. 'That's good. I have some questions I'd like to ask them.'

'Doctor, are you sure that's a good idea?' asked Clara.

'Not at all.'

'They are coming,' Jem repeated loudly.

At the centre of the bridge a blue glow had appeared in the air. It grew brighter and expanded, forming the shape of a tall, humanoid figure in long robes and a hood. Two others appeared on either side of the first, similarly robed. As they materialised their features became visible: long, birdlike faces with large, dark eyes. They stared unblinkingly at the people gathered before them.

'We are here,' said Jem, as if she was in a trance. 'We are the Phaeron.'

We are the Phaeron

They didn't speak aloud but the voices boomed in the minds of everyone in the room. Clara heard and understood, even though the Phaeron never actually spoke, and judging by the reactions of those around her, they all understood as well. It wasn't painful but every word seemed to fill her mind when the Phaeron spoke, blotting out every other conscious thought.

We are the Phaeron

Tibby Vent stood directly in front of the central figure and cleared her throat. 'Can you hear me?'

Yes

Tibby gasped, pressing her fist into her lip with barely suppressed glee.

'Remarkable,' said the Doctor.

'Are they actually here, then? The Phaeron?' Clara asked him quietly.

'I'm not sure.'

'How are we communicating?'

'They're using Jem as a sort of telepathic loudhailer,' said the Doctor.

'Will she be OK?'

'I don't know. Let's find out.' The Doctor stepped up onto the central podium to face the Phaeron. He took a deep breath before speaking. 'I'm the Doctor. Pleased to meet you at last.'

We know you Time Lord

The Doctor looked a little startled. 'You do? Oh. That's… interesting. Good. I've not had the pleasure?'

We are the Phaeron

'Yes, getting that, thank you very much. How are you communicating with us? I mean, I know you're using our friend Jem here as a kind of mouthpiece, and I do hope you're treating her gently, but given that your entire race is extinct… how can we be talking to you now?'

We are the Phaeron

'OK, I think we've hit a snag,' said the Doctor.

'They sound like a recording,' said Clara.

The Doctor clicked his fingers. 'That's because it *is* a recording! It's a message – left for us here at the centre of the *Carthage*.'

'Don't be ridiculous,' said Tibby crossly. 'You can't talk to a recording.'

'It depends how sophisticated the recording is.' The Doctor quickly scanned the Phaeron with his sonic screwdriver. 'These are perceptual-telepathic messages from the Phaeron. Interactive recordings working off an artificial intelligence. There are no living Phaeron, Tibby. I'm sorry. What we're seeing are still ghosts.'

We have been waiting

We are trapped

'So they're stuck here as well,' the Doctor said. 'Isn't that interesting?'

'What happened?' asked Clara.

In the time of the Phaeron, all the stars and the planets and their moons belonged to us

'Modest too,' said the Doctor.

The universe was ours

There were no others

Our time was Perfect

We were Perfect
The Doctor pulled a face. 'Not so modest now.'
We travelled on the Phaeron Roads
'Old news,' said Clara.
The universe was ours
There were no others
Then the Imperfection came
'Oh, that doesn't sound good.'
'The Imperfection?' repeated the Doctor. 'We've been hearing a lot about that now. What happened?'
It spoiled the Phaeron
'What are they talking about, Doctor?' asked Tibby. 'I don't understand.'
It was Imperfect
'It was *evil*,' realised the Doctor. 'Think about it: the Phaeron practically owned the universe. They were here before anyone else. "There were no others." It was a *paradise*. The Phaeron had built their own Eden. A perfect civilisation. Imagine that! No hunger, no poverty, no envy, free travel and health care, unlimited data usage and free Wi-Fi. They could go anywhere they liked, do anything they liked. There was nothing to stop them, nothing to interfere.'
'The whole universe was their oyster, you mean?' Clara said.
'A garden of delights. Paradise. Eden.' The Doctor gave the Phaeron a baleful look. 'Until the serpent came.'
The Phaeron stared back, their eyes empty black orbs and completely unreadable.
The Phaeron… craved… the Imperfection
It spoiled the Phaeron

'But what *was* it?' Clara wondered.

'Oh I think we can guess,' said the Doctor. 'Something too tempting to resist, too attractive to ignore? Something that not even the Phaeron could rise above. Something they *craved*.'

Clara suddenly understood. 'It was the Glamour, wasn't it?'

It was Imperfect

It spoiled the Phaeron

'But what happened? What did they do?' asked Tibby.

The Phaeron craved the Imperfection

'Oh yes,' the Doctor said. 'I'm beginning to see it now all right. The Glamour came. The Phaeron fell under its spell. And everything went bad.'

'What, everything?' Tibby sounded sceptical. 'It destroyed the whole Phaeron civilisation?'

'They were *perfect*, Professor. And that means they were vulnerable – to imperfection, as they call it. Think of it like a virus. They had no defences. Perhaps everything was so good for them they stopped thinking of anything else. They stopped believing that there might be things that weren't perfect, that wanted to harm them and could harm them. Or perhaps, one day, there was a Phaeron who wasn't perfect. One who learned to take advantage of the goodwill of the others, one that tricked them and used them and set themselves above the rest.'

'You mean the Glamour could simply be a rogue Phaeron?'

'Like the Devil – a fallen angel, thrown out of Heaven,' Clara realised.

'It's not impossible. It would explain a great deal – most people see the Glamour as very attractive and desirable. Perfect, perhaps. They would do anything to possess it – and thus it possesses them.'

Clara looked at the Phaeron wraiths again and felt sorry for them. They just stood, impassive, their long beaklike faces and dark, liquid eyes seemed quite helpless and forlorn.

We tried to make it Perfect
It could not be made Perfect
It was Imperfect
The Phaeron disposed of the Imperfection

'They destroyed it?' queried Tibby.

'How?' asked the Doctor.

The Phaeron disposed of the Imperfection

'So they didn't *destroy* it. Such an enlightened race would never tolerate capital punishment,' the Doctor noted approvingly. 'They caught the Glamour and *disposed* of it.'

'Where?'

Deep Time

'Deep time?' echoed Clara.

'Now I see,' said the Doctor. He pressed the palms of his hands together and paced around the *Carthage* bridge. 'The Phaeron drilled a hole in time into this lost planet as a dungeon for the Glamour. That's how they were planning to dispose of it – send it way back in time, back to before the Phaeron even existed.'

'The Phaeron had time travel?'

'Not as such. But they had the ability to make holes in space-time, remember. The Phaeron Roads. They could travel around the universe using a vast network of wormholes. But that's no way to get rid of the Glamour, so they built a wormhole that only existed in one spatial dimension. A hole through time – going backwards, deeper and deeper.'

'Like a dungeon,' said Vent.

'Or a well,' said Clara. 'You said we were stuck in a well, looking up at the sky.'

'Exactly. And this is it. We're in the Phaerons' time dungeon!'

The last road of the Phaeron
The final journey
Deep Time

'But we can get out, can't we?' said Balfour. 'We've got the *Carthage*. It works. Hobbo says it can still fly.'

'I reckon it might,' Hobbo agreed. 'With a bit of luck and a fair wind.'

The final journey

'That's why the *Carthage* is stuck here!' the Doctor exclaimed suddenly, smacking one fist into the palm of his other hand. 'It must have crashed into the Phaeron vessel in the middle of the wormhole as it was disposing of the Glamour.'

'But I thought all this happened eons ago,' argued Tibby. 'The *Carthage* disappeared only a hundred years ago.'

'But the Phaeron were drilling a time well into this planet. They were using the last of their wormholes, remember. They'd closed everything else down except for this one – their *final journey*.'

'You mean they were taking the Glamour with them?'

'Yes…' The Doctor looked suddenly pale as realisation dawned. 'It was a suicide mission.'

The final journey
Deep Time

Chapter

19

'Suicide mission?' The words felt thick and ugly in Clara's mouth and she felt her stomach lurch a little at the thought. Suddenly, laundry and marking had never seemed so compelling.

'There was only one way to be sure the Glamour goes all the way down the deepest well they could dig,' said the Doctor. 'By taking it there themselves.'

'But still. Suicide.'

'You heard them,' said Tibby sadly. 'The final journey.'

'But we can still leave, can't we?' asked Balfour. 'In the *Carthage,* I mean.'

'I've just done a few checks an' I'd say it was touch and go,' said Hobbo. She was leaning against one of the controls panels, arms folded. A sudden spasm of sadness crossed her face and she frowned. 'I'd feel better if Mitch was here.'

'But what are we going to do?' said Balfour, looking more and more worried. 'I mean – you heard them. They're on a suicide mission to the dawn of time. We don't want to join them, do we?'

'Isn't there anything we can do, Hobbo?' asked Tibby.

'I'd have to try an' start her up first,' Hobbo said. 'I couldn't say for sure until we tried.'

'I don't much fancy the one-way option, either,' said Clara. She turned to the Doctor. 'Come on. How can we get this spaceship flying again? You always think of something.'

The Doctor pursed his lips. 'Well, if we had the TARDIS, things would be a lot simpler, of course.'

'But we don't,' said Balfour.

'A miracle sure would come in handy right now,' Hobbo said.

'But we don't have the TARDIS,' repeated Balfour.

'We haven't seen the TARDIS since we left the *Alexandria*,' agreed Clara. 'And you said the signal was gone, Doctor.'

'Yes, I did.' The Doctor's eyes grew hooded. 'But that was before I knew the Phaeron were still here – if only in spirit.'

We know you Time Lord
We remember the coming of the Time Lords

'I was rather hoping you didn't,' said the Doctor.

We remember the coming of the New Universe
The passing of the Time of the Phaeron

'That was before my time, if you see what I mean,' the Doctor said. 'Way before. The Time Lords changed. They fought their own wars and Gallifrey was lost. Perhaps lost for ever.'

Gallifrey knew the Imperfection

'If you mean the Glamour, then yes. It was a powerful force for evil. The Time Lords could not allow it to influence the universe in the way it wished. And with your power, the Glamour – the Imperfection – could have caused great damage to later civilisations.'

We know this

'Oh. Right. Sorry.'

Gallifrey warned the Phaeron

The Doctor looked shocked. 'What? But I thought the Time Lords forced you to close down the Phaeron Roads to stop the Glamour. I thought they caused your destruction.'

The Time Lords could not destroy us

'Ah.' The Doctor turned to the others. 'See? I said they were more powerful than I thought.'

The Phaeron will deal with their own Imperfection

'But even if that means destroying yourselves in the process?'

The final journey

Deep Time

'That's awful,' said Tibby softly. 'They killed themselves just to rid the universe of the Glamour?'

'Self-sacrifice on a cosmic level,' the Doctor said.

'It's so sad,' Clara whispered. She looked at the shimmering blue figures, and suddenly they seemed neither frightening nor mysterious – just tragic.

'*Noblesse oblige*,' the Doctor said. 'They were the perfect race. They did the right thing by the universe, whatever the consequences. They created the Glamour, what they saw as an Imperfection, and so they dealt with it. Or, at least, they're trying to.'

The final journey must be completed

'But they're struck. The *Carthage* flew straight into

their last wormhole as they were about to dispose the Glamour. They've been trapped here ever since. And the Glamour is still at large, flitting around the universe causing mayhem.'

'So the mission failed? It was all for nothing?'

'Not quite. The Glamour is the Imperfection, remember. It's part of the Phaeron race. To us it looks like something perfect, something we desire more than anything. That's how it uses people. But our perfection is their *imperfection*. It's a part of them, it's tied to them – that's why they're having to go on the final journey with it.'

'So if the mission is completed, the Glamour goes with them?'

'Whether it likes it or not, yes.'

You must leave before the final journey is complete

The Doctor clasped his hands together and frowned. 'Well, that's very kind of you. And we would leave – except that we have no means of doing so.'

We know you Time Lord

'That is very flattering, but…'

We know you… Doctor

The words of the Phaeron boomed in Clara's mind and suddenly took on fresh meaning. The Doctor's eyes were glinting like diamonds as he turned to face the Phaeron. 'Yes! You *do* know me. You *must* know me. Because *you* have my TARDIS, don't you?'

The Phaeron will make the final journey

Behind the Phaeron, a fresh blue glow appeared in the gloom, growing into the shape of a large, tall box with a lamp on top. Doors and windows appeared in the shimmering rectangle and the words 'POLICE BOX' shone out from the roof.

'It's a gift,' said the Doctor. His words were tinged by sadness and humility, and he closed his eyes in relief. 'They're grateful to the Time Lords for pointing out their own Imperfection.'

Eventually the blue light faded, and with it the Phaeron also disappeared, like moonbeams behind a cloud. The bridge was suddenly darker; quiet and empty.

'Erm, Doctor…' said Clara. 'Is the TARDIS all right?'

The Doctor's eyes snapped open. The TARDIS stood proudly in the centre of the room, but the journey seemed to have taken its toll. The paintwork was cracked, peeling off in long strips. The frosted windows where dark and rimmed with dust and grime.

'Looks like it's been in the wars, Doc,' said Hobbo.

Ashen-faced, the Doctor slowly approached the police box. He touched one of the doors, felt the curling blue paintwork crumble. 'Well…' he said, very quietly. 'It's been a while, hasn't it? How many billions of years have you been waiting, I wonder?'

Clara swallowed awkwardly as the Doctor traced his long, trembling fingers over the TARDIS woodwork, tracing the old, cracked sign on the hatch that contained the telephone. 'How can it have aged like that if it's been going backwards in time?' she wondered.

'Time is relative, Clara. The TARDIS has been tracking back to the source of the time fluxes, the here and now. She must have taken the long road. The Phaeron weren't to know. They did their best.'

'We can't all fit in there anyway,' said Balfour.

'We can,' Clara said. 'It's bigger inside. Much bigger.'

Balfour shrugged. 'If you say so.'

'It must have dematerialised when it went over the cliff with the *Alexandria*,' said the Doctor. 'The Phaeron probably sensed its presence in the local time-space continuum and picked up it. They've kept it ever since.'

'But… it's so old.'

'That doesn't mean anything to the Phaeron, Clara. They exist outside and at one with time and space.'

Clara had never seen the Doctor looking so lost. He rested his head against the TARDIS and closed his eyes. Clara reached out and touched the time machine. It felt as cold as a gravestone. There was no faint vibration, no humming sound. It was lifeless.

'Should we go inside?' she asked. The idea made her feel strangely anxious now.

Slowly, heavily, the Doctor drew the TARDIS key from his pocket and inserted it in the lock. At first it was too stiff to turn. But eventually the lock scraped open and the Doctor pushed the door. It creaked loudly on corroded hinges.

It was dark inside. That was the first thing that properly frightened Clara. The outside of the TARDIS was tough, she knew – practically indestructible, the Doctor would say. She guessed it could survive a fair bit of aging. It was a time machine after all.

But inside was different. The inside was supposed to be inviolate. Untouchable. But time had got inside the TARDIS and ravaged it with a ferocity that took Clara's breath away. There was not a single light shining on the central console, or any of the surrounding instrument panels. The central column was dark, the glass filaments inside were cloudy and cracked. Normally they would be blazing with a warm orange glow, a fireside glow, welcoming and full of energy and promise. But now there was nothing but emptiness and silence.

Her footsteps echoed on the metal floor as she followed the Doctor down the short gangplank to the control area. He walked slowly around the console, letting his fingers drag over the darkened controls, drawing thick lines through the dust.

'What's happened?' Clara asked, appalled.

'The TARDIS is dead, Clara,' the Doctor replied.

'It's not your fault.'

'Isn't it?' The Doctor looked bleakly at her. His eyes were like chips of blue ice. 'I brought us here. You, me and the TARDIS. I knew it was going to be dangerous. I said so, right at the start.'

'It's always dangerous. Well, nearly always. But usually...'

'Usually we escape. We survive.' The Doctor sighed. 'Well, you needn't worry there. We can still do that. There's still the *Carthage*, remember.'

'I know, but Hobbo said it may not fly.'

'Oh, I'm sure she'll find a way. She has to. Otherwise we'll all end up like this, eventually.' The Doctor tapped a knuckle on the TARDIS console. And then, with sudden and explosive fury he smashed his fist down on the metal. He saw Clara flinch as the noise of it echoed around the room and smiled sadly. 'I'm sorry. I shouldn't have done that.'

'It's all right, really...'

'No, I think I've broken a finger,' the Doctor held up his hand with a grimace of pain.

Clara took his hand gently, and closed her fingers around his. His hand felt cold and she thought she could detect a slight tremble. Suddenly his skin looked pale and thin, like an old man's. 'I'm sorry,' she said.

'So am I.'

'Hey, Doc,' said Hobbo. She stood in the doorway, poking her head into the console room. 'I tried firin' up the *Carthage* an' guess what? Looks like we might have a ship after all.'

The Doctor nodded absently. 'Good, good. That's good.'

'Maybe the TARDIS will be better if we get her away from the time well,' suggested Clara. 'Maybe once we're free of the *Carthage* and the Phaeron, it'll get better. You know, regenerate or something.'

The Doctor nodded absently. 'Yes, possibly,' he agreed, but there was no conviction in his voice.

'And we can't just leave the others anyway, can we?'

'Others?'

'They're going to need you to help get the *Carthage* working, aren't they?'

'Yes, probably.'

She led him away from the console and out of the TARDIS. She was careful to shut the door behind them, wincing as the hinges squealed in protest.

*

Hobbo was busy at the main control stations, lying on her back with her head inside an inspection hatch. Jem was sitting in one of the flight seats. Balfour was helping Tibby clear away cobwebs and weeds from the surfaces.

'It looks like we're good to go,' Balfour said.

Tibby glanced at him uncertainly. To the Doctor she said, 'I'm sorry about your TARDIS.'

'It's… OK,' the Doctor said heavily. He seemed to be moving slowly, as if he was in a dream, thought Clara. Or a nightmare. He looked back at the husk of the TARDIS and closed his eyes, as if in pain.

There were lights blinking on all the *Carthage* instruments now and it looked more like the bridge of a spaceship than a mausoleum. Clara thought she could detect a vibration beneath her feet as power started to flood through the vessel. More lights came on in the overhead consoles. The entire ship began to feel warmer and brighter as more systems came online.

'I wish Dan was with us,' Jem said as she ran through a sequence of pre-flight checks. 'He'd know a lot more about this than me.'

'No kiddin',' said Hobbo as she sat up. There was a streak of dirt on her face. 'I keep thinkin': what would Mitch do with this?'

'Do you think you can fly the *Carthage*?' Clara asked them.

'Shouldn't be a problem. It's not dissimilar to the *Alexandria*. Blast-off is automated. I just hope the autorepair systems are back online.'

Hobbo snapped shut the inspection hatch. 'They're all

firin' and fixin' as we speak. It's all systems go. Quite the old trooper, this ship.'

'So are we good to go?' asked Balfour impatiently.

'Yep,' said Hobbo. 'We don't have a lot of power so every second we wait costs us more.'

'Right,' Balfour said, clapping his hands. 'Everyone find a seat and strap in. Let's go.'

'Let's not,' said the Doctor.

There was a sharp, unexpected silence as the Doctor's words echoed around the flight deck. Everybody's eyes turned to look at him. He stood in the centre of the room, arms folded, resolute.

Balfour frowned. 'What? Strap in, Doctor. You heard Hobbo: it could be a bumpy ride.'

'Oh, I know that,' said the Doctor. 'But I'm not going to make the journey. None of us are.'

Chapter

20

'What do you mean?' Balfour looked confused, almost irritated.

'Doctor?' said Clara, uncertain.

The Doctor walked slowly around the bridge, circling Balfour. His eyes were hard. 'We're not leaving the time well,' he said.

'What are you talking about, Doctor?' asked Balfour. 'Look around you! We have the perfect opportunity to leave this place! Stop delaying!'

'The perfect opportunity?' repeated the Doctor. He looked around the bridge. 'Yes, it is, isn't it? An old, crashed spaceship that's still fully functional. What luck!'

'Doctor,' said Balfour, forcing patience into his voice, 'we're running out of time...'

'Are we? I thought we were stuck in time. Lodged like a fishbone in its throat.' The Doctor looked indignant. 'Time's been coughing for eternity on this planet, trying to dislodge the blockage. That's what all those time fluctuations were – poor old Mother Time, gagging and choking to death.'

The spaceship engines were now a deep, background rumble, like thunder before a storm. Clara said, 'Doctor...'

The Doctor ignored her as his voice hardened. 'The *Carthage* entered the wormhole and smashed straight into the Phaerons' ship, fusing a discrete area of the space-time continuum so that neither could move. Which means the Phaeron never actually completed their journey, as we know. Which means the Glamour is still free to roam – until that journey is completed.'

'Yes, we know that. So let's help them do it,' said Balfour eagerly. 'Let's help them finish their mission. If we leave in the *Carthage* right now, the blockage will be cleared.'

'The blockage will be cleared, yes,' agreed the Doctor.

'We can all survive,' Balfour added.

'No.' The Doctor shook his head. 'No, I'm afraid we can't. The *Carthage* isn't going to fly – not properly. You might get enough power to blast off – but that will be it. If we're lucky it'll explode in deep space and every one of us will be instantly vaporised.'

'And if we're unlucky?' asked Clara, incredulous.

'Hull integrity will be maintained but life support will fail and we'll all asphyxiate. Slowly.'

There was an awkward silence for a few seconds.

'But the ship is workin',' said Hobbo. 'It's fine.'

'Is it?' The Doctor whirled and fixed the young engineer with his fiercest stare. 'Do you really believe that, Hobbo? Oh, look – everything's working fine and it's all shiny and great!' The Doctor turned to look at the others, each in turn, his eyebrows raised like a teacher challenging his class. 'Is that what you really think?'

'Well, it is bit fortunate, I suppose,' Clara said, uncertainly. 'But…'

'But it ain't possible,' said Hobbo. 'It just ain't.'

'Then look again, Hobbo,' said the Doctor gently. 'All of you, look again. Does this look like a spaceship to you?'

Clara blinked and looked around the bridge once more. She could see the control panels, the flashing lights on the instruments. She could feel the hum of the engines, sense the power contained inside the ship. She wanted to say yes but something was stopping her. Something at the back of her mind, like the distant ringing of a bell. Something in the Doctor's voice. Something she trusted, almost more than she trusted herself.

She looked again. The control panels were like fossilised lumps of rock, gnarled and cracked and overgrown with weeds. There were no flashing lights, only thin, grey spiders creeping stealthily through the debris. There was no vibration, no engine noise, just a fetid, rotting stench and tendrils of mist creeping across the floor.

'The *Carthage* isn't going anywhere,' said the Doctor.

Tibby had been watching the entire exchange with increasing anxiety. She cleared her throat, the sound was awkward in the silence. She looked at Balfour and said, 'You're not Ray Balfour… are you?'

'You're mad,' said Balfour.

'You're the Glamour,' said the Doctor.

With a sudden roar of anger, Balfour threw the Doctor across the bridge. Then he lunged for the *Carthage*'s flight controls again, scrabbling through the dirt to ignite the engines.

'Don't let him blast off!' yelled the Doctor.

Jem tried to grab Balfour but he had the strength of a wild animal, shoving her roughly away. Hunched over the controls, he began to hit buried switches and activator panels with a manic urgency. Grime-covered lights flickered and long forgotten circuits sparked into life. An unnatural rumble shook the bridge as if an ancient beast was being woken from a long sleep. Cracks appeared all over the room, sending clouds of dust tumbling to the floor. Metal glinted beneath the calcified shell like the bones glimpsed through ruptured flesh.

'I'll take you all with me!' Balfour grated through gnashing teeth. Spittle flew from his lips. 'I'll take you all with me!'

The Doctor dug his long fingers into the nape of Balfour's neck and squeezed hard. Balfour bared his teeth in pain, his eyes rolling madly, but there was no moving him. The *Carthage* began to vibrate as if a gigantic swarm of angry hornets was crawling around the bridge, searching for a way in.

Clara and Hobbo took hold of Balfour, each trying to pull one of his clawed hands from the controls, but he seemed to be able to fight both of them and the Doctor.

'Don't let him take off!' the Doctor screamed again. His voice was almost lost in the roar of the ancient engines as they were forced into action.

There was a sudden, bright flash of purple light which arced across the room and struck Balfour directly between the shoulder blades. He threw his head back with a gasp and then sank to his knees.

Tibby Vent stood holding the ion bonder out in front of her in two hands, her face stricken. 'I'm sorry!' she said. 'It's all I could think of!'

'It's a good job you did, too,' said Hobbo, out of breath. She pushed Balfour away from the controls and the man landed on all fours, saliva drooling from his mouth.

Jem stared at him with a look of fascination and horror. 'That's not Balfour,' she whispered.

'Don't look at him,' ordered the Doctor. 'Don't look at him, any of you.'

Clara obediently looked away. She stared at the Doctor instead, although she was still aware of Balfour, hunched on the floor, whimpering like a dog.

'Tibby and Jem are right; that's *not* Raymond Balfour,' the Doctor said, straightening his jacket. 'It's something called the Glamour, taking his form. The Imperfection that the Phaeron are trying to bury. It's trying to escape from its captors by hitching a ride out of the time well.'

'But I thought you said the *Carthage* couldn't fly?' said Tibby.

'It can't – at least not far enough. This ship just isn't space worthy any more. Millions of years of entropic decay can't just be shrugged off in a few minutes.'

Hobbo looked bewildered. 'But I really believed it could fly. We all did.'

The Doctor nodded. 'That's the Glamour at work, doing what it does best – appealing to your desires, taking what you want to believe and amplifying and controlling it. It absorbs every wish you have, your heart's desire, and throws it right back to you. We all wanted to believe there was a way out of the time well. We all wanted to believe that the *Carthage*, having been lost here and waiting for millions of years, could suddenly be made space worthy and fly us all safely out of here. How romantic. How convenient! How *impossible*.'

'But what are we going to do?' asked Clara, trying to keep the desperation out of her voice. She could feel her heart hammering in her chest. The *Carthage* was shaking itself to pieces around them and there was no way out. 'How can we escape?'

'In the TARDIS, of course.'

Clara turned to where the TARDIS stood at the back of the room. The police box was resplendently solid and blue, without any sign of peeling paintwork or fungal growths. The windows were clear. The sign over the doors shone with its usual steady reassurance.

'It's back again,' Clara said, her eyes moist at the sight. 'The way it should be.'

'The way it always was. The Glamour didn't want to leave in the TARDIS. It wouldn't be able to maintain the illusion of itself inside the TARDIS. *Its true form and intent would be instantly revealed.* No, it had to convince us not to use the TARDIS, and that the *Carthage* was the only way.'

'Well,' Clara sniffed, wiping her eyes, 'it convinced me.'

'When did you realise, Doctor?' asked Tibby.

'As soon as the TARDIS was returned to me by the Phaeron. I didn't see what you saw. The TARDIS and I are too close to be fooled by that kind of rubbish, and besides – it's a *time machine*. Do you think a few billion years could even touch it? Look at her! Big, bold, beautiful and blue.

She's never let me down.'

'But...' Clara said.

'Why did I play along with the Glamour's illusion?' The Doctor's deep eyes twinkled for a moment. 'I had to force the Glamour to show itself. At that point, I didn't know who it actually was.'

'I knew,' said Tibby quietly. 'I knew something wasn't right. It wasn't Ray Balfour. It wasn't anything like the man I... the man I know.'

'I'm afraid it became all too obvious in the end,' admitted the Doctor.

'But if the *Carthage* had taken off?' wondered Hobbo. 'What would have happened?'

'With luck it might have escaped the time well, but its engines would have failed and life support with it. It would have become a derelict, adrift in deep space. And you would all have perished.'

'What about the Glamour?'

'The Glamour doesn't need air to breathe, or food or water. It could survive for a thousand years, a hundred thousand – for all eternity, perhaps. But someone or something would have picked it up eventually, probably searching for their heart's desire. The Glamour would have become everything they wanted, and more. And then it would feed on those desires, and grow stronger, and more powerful and influential.' The Doctor looked sombre. 'The worst of the Phaeron would have been left at large in an unsuspecting universe.'

'What about the real Ray Balfour though?' asked Tibby. 'Where is he?'

'I dread to think. Maybe we should ask the Glamour.'

But when the Doctor looked down there was no sign of the thing that had taken Raymond Balfour's form. 'Where did he go?'

'I don't know,' Clara said. 'You told us not to look at him!'

'Doctor, Jem's gone too,' said Hobbo, pointing to the empty pilot's chair.

The Doctor's face fell into an expression of horror. 'Oh no. That's not good. That's not good at all.'

'We have to find her,' Clara said.

Jem followed the limping figure along the darkened corridor. He moved slowly, with an irregular gait, and was clearly injured or unwell. Jem didn't know where he was headed, but he seemed to be leading her deeper into the ship. The noise of the *Carthage*'s engines was growing louder all the time. They growled under the floor, vibrating everything in a teeth-rattling jangle.

'Where are you going?' she asked, hurrying after the shadowy figure.

He didn't pause, didn't turn around. He just kept limping, dragging one foot behind him, holding on to the walls for support. Every time Jem thought she was about to catch up, he disappeared around the next corner, or down a flight of steps. At one point, she had to force her way through a curtain of vegetation that had grown up the walls and along the ceiling to hang down in dry, ragged tendrils. Beyond that was a larger room, full of thick cylinders like stacks of giant coins. The noise in here was worse, and it felt as if the whole world was shaking. Smoke curled around the base of the cylinders as they pulsed with blue light.

There was a figure lying on the floor, curled up. Jem saw the tangle of blond hair and realised it was Raymond Balfour. Perhaps he was dead. It didn't matter. Balfour wasn't who she was looking for.

'Where are you?' Jem called out.

A shadow moved behind one of the cylinders.

'I know you're there,' Jem said. 'Why don't you come out? I know who you are.'

The shadow hesitated, turned. Walked slowly forwards, into the light of the cylinders.

'I always knew who you were,' Jem said.

'I didn't realise it was you,' said Dan Laker. He looked tired, haggard, and there were bruises on his face. He was still wearing his spacesuit, although it looked damaged and of course the helmet was missing – buried in the snow a million years hence. Laker held himself painfully, hunched over, hurt, still limping.

'Did you think I'd ever leave you?' Jem asked, stepping closer.

'No,' he replied. 'Not ever.'

He came forward, straightening a little. In the flickering light his bruises looked less obvious. He brushed a hand through his hair in the way she remembered and smiled gently at her. 'I've missed you,' Jem said.

'I never meant to hurt you,' Laker told her. 'The Phaeron took me from the *Alexandria* as it went over the cliff. I never thought I'd see you again.'

Jem stepped forward again, close enough to touch him. The nearer she got, the better he looked; the bruises faded, the cuts disappeared. He stood taller and stronger.

'The *Carthage* is going to explode,' Jem said. 'You have to get off this ship.'

'Let me come with you,' he said, reaching out.

'Jem!' The Doctor's voice rang out clearly from behind her. 'Don't let him touch you.'

She turned to find the Doctor and Clara behind her, at the entrance to the engine room. Tibby and Hobbo were with them. Tibby ran to where Ray Balfour lay on the floor and examined him. 'He's breathing. He's alive. Thank God!'

Hobbo helped Tibby lift him. He looked groggy but unharmed. 'What's happening?'

'Somethin's about to hit the fan,' said Hobbo. 'Get ready to duck.'

The Doctor had his hands out towards Jem, his fingers splayed wide, as if he could somehow control her like a puppeteer. 'Wait, Jem. Think about this carefully.'

'I have,' she replied.

Laker recoiled, backing a little way into the shadows.

'Leave us alone,' Jem said. 'Please. Go.'

'But that's not Dan Laker,' Clara told her. 'It's the Glamour. It's making you believe it's really Dan, but it's not.'

'Don't listen to them, Jem,' said Laker.

One of the engine stacks cracked open and a sun-bright flame flickered within, sending long fingers of light out to touch every surface.

'The *Carthage* engines are overheatin',' yelled Hobbo.

The grinding throb of ancient machinery had reached a crescendo while they were talking. 'Those astronic thrusters have been powerin' up for literally the first time in eons!'

The Doctor, silhouetted in the madly wavering glare, strode forward and grasped Jem by the arm. 'We must leave now!'

'No, Doctor,' Jem had to shout over the noise. 'I have to be here! I'm staying with Dan!'

'That's not Dan Laker!' the Doctor repeated fiercely.

The ground shook suddenly and another engine stack split from top to bottom. Blazing fingers of energy groped around the room, found nearby stacks, began to dig in. The Doctor started forward but a brilliant arc of white energy crackled between him and Jem. Clara grabbed hold of the Doctor and pulled him back, yelling for him to keep away.

Jem held out her hand to Laker. He took her in his arms and smiled at the Doctor and Clara.

'No!' Clara screamed.

'*It's not Dan Laker,*' the Doctor said again, his voice full of despair.

'*I know,*' Jem said. And then she tightened her grip on Laker, digging her fingers in hard to make sure he couldn't get away.

A blue glow enveloped them both, tendrils of energy flickering out to connect with the engine stacks. The glow deepened, and out of the blue stepped three tall, hooded figures.

'The Phaeron!' Clara gasped.

We make the final journey

The Doctor looked astonished. 'No, you can't…'

'I have to make sure,' Jem said, still holding Laker tight. 'I have to make sure the Phaeron take it with them. We have to go into deep time together.'

The Phaeron reached out to Laker and Jem. Laker snarled, twisting suddenly this way and that, but Jem held him fast in her arms. Laker's face elongated, becoming aquiline and pointed like a beak, and his eyes disappeared into wide black holes on either side of a skinless head. Clara had once seen a crow's skull and it did not look dissimilar. The sharp beak cracked open and the shoulders drew up behind it, suddenly hunched and scrawny. The eye sockets filled with balls of squirming grey things and a thin, keening wail rose above the thundering roar of the engines.

And then the Phaeron drew back into the blue glow, taking the keening thing with them, and Jem also, and then more engine stacks split and the unleashed energy whipped around the room.

'For pity's sake, get outta there!' Hobbo grabbed hold of both the Doctor and Clara and pulled them away. They turned and, together with Tibby and Balfour, they ran for their lives as the *Carthage* disintegrated around them.

Chapter

21

The *Carthage* was, in real terms at least, now hundreds of millions of years old. It didn't take long to break apart when the astronic engines burst under the sudden strain of ignition. A river of superhot plasma surged through the corridors and decks, pushing an incandescent wall of flame before it and leaving nothing but molten slag behind it.

They sprinted into the TARDIS with the flames scorching their heels and the police box door snapped shut with a bang as the plasma hit. Burning energy engulfed the time ship in a storm of charged ions. The last vestiges of the incinerating atmosphere carried with it the final roar of the explosion, and a faint wheezing and groaning as the police box started to dematerialise. The ablation of the plasma stream disappeared a moment before the *Carthage* itself turned into an expanding cloud of accelerated atoms.

Out of the dazzling firestorm shot a tiny speck of blue matter, spinning end over end, the lamp on its roof flashing busily as it faded from the material universe and slipped into that mysterious vortex where time and space are one.

*

The Doctor clung to the control console, one hand darting here and there among the levers and switches. The brilliant orange filaments in the glass column at the centre of the console rose gently up and down, casting a warm, homely glow on his old face. Above him, the giant time rotors turned this way and that as the TARDIS calculated its exact position in the space-time continuum.

Clara picked herself off the floor. Tibby Vent and Hobbo were also getting to their feet, and so was Raymond Balfour. They all looked as shaky as Clara felt.

'We made it, then,' Balfour said, holding on to the console for support.

'Of course we did,' said the Doctor, finally stepping back from the controls and flexing his long fingers. He laced them together and cracked his knuckles. 'Never in doubt.'

Clara gave him a look but said nothing. Her skin was tingling and there was a burnt smell in the air. She guessed that they had all got a little singed near the end.

The Doctor swung the TARDIS monitor screen around and tapped it. 'Look at that.'

They peered at the display. It showed a profusion of overlapping concentric circles and elegant hexagonal equations. At the centre of the diagram was a bright sphere of coruscating energy, disappearing into a long, swirling vortex.

'Is that the Phaeron ship?' Clara wondered.

'Yes.'

'It's gone,' said Tibby. 'Taking the Glamour with it.'

'Like a spider down a plughole,' the Doctor said. He switched the monitor off with a flourish. 'Gone for ever.'

'But Jem…' said Clara.

'She had to do it. She was the only one who could make sure the Glamour went down with the Phaeron ship.'

'We must've taken quite a radiation hit when the *Carthage* engines blew,' Hobbo said.

The Doctor waved a hand dismissively. 'Not a problem. The moment you stepped into the TARDIS that would have been dealt with. No ill effects. Just a few scorch marks.'

'This ship of yours really *is* a miracle, ain't it, Doc?' asked Hobbo. She looked around her in pure amazement.

'Not a miracle,' said the Doctor. 'Just a—'

'Mockery of time and space, yeah, I get it.'

The Doctor frowned. 'Actually I was going to say a superb example of relative dimensional engineering.'

Balfour said, 'We ought to thank you, Doctor… but we lost so many people. Jem gave her life to make sure the Glamour was destroyed. Tanya was killed. Mitch was killed. And Marco…'

The Doctor regarded him severely. 'I said at the beginning that your mission was dangerous. I wasn't joking.'

'I should have paid more attention,' said Balfour sadly. He looked haggard, almost desolate. 'I should have abandoned the mission at the outset.'

'On my word?' The Doctor was scandalised. 'Don't be ridiculous. The *Alexandria* was a beautiful ship and a bold adventure. Just think: we travelled down the last Phaeron wormhole. We discovered a new planet, lost in the intergalactic void. We found the *Carthage*. We met the Phaeron themselves! And, most importantly, we helped stop the Glamour once and for all. Believe me, the universe is a better place without it.'

The TARDIS stood on the main concourse overlooking the public docking bays of Far Station. Clara watched in amazement as humans, aliens, robots and things she couldn't even classify wandered around, hurrying towards departure gates and waiting space vehicles or just taking in the sights. It could be bewildering. It could be frightening. But it was never anything less than amazing.

'Good of you to drop us off,' Balfour said to the Doctor. He was standing with Hobbo and Tibby in front of the TARDIS.

The Doctor was hanging out of the police box door. 'Well I can't have you all cluttering up the TARDIS. You've seen what it's like inside. There's barely enough room for Clara.'

Balfour smiled. 'It may take me a while to get over the experience, Doctor, but I'm glad I had it. I've learned a lot about myself – and about other people. In fact, I've already spoken to Tibby and Hobbo about another idea: Tibby says she's gained a new insight into some of the Phaeron ruins in other parts of the galaxy. We're thinking of buying a new starship and—'

'Don't tell me any more,' said the Doctor, raising a hand in surrender.

Clara smiled and nudged him. 'I think there's a bit more to it than looking for some old ruins, Doctor.'

'What are you talking about?' The Doctor looked at Tibby and Balfour, and suddenly noticed that they were holding hands. 'What are you doing that for? Holding hands like that. What's it for?'

'We're together now, Doctor,' said Tibby happily.

'I can see that. You're right in front of me. But why are you holding hands like that?'

'I'll explain later,' Clara told him.

'We thought you and Clara might like to come with us,' Balfour said.

'There's a particular item on Ursa Minor,' said Tibby. 'It's a genuine Phaeron icon. It demands study.'

The Doctor sighed. 'If you want my advice, and of course you do, then leave it well alone. Forget all about Ursa Minor. Forget about the Phaeron. Forget about anything that *demands* study, or looks too good to resist, or appears perfect. Go and discover something else.' The Doctor paused, stared at their clasped hands for a long moment, and then added, 'Like each other, for example.'

'What a good idea,' said Clara.

The Doctor held open the TARDIS door. 'Clara, come on. Stop interfering. Home time.'

Tibby began to protest, but the Doctor held up a finger for silence and fixed them with a dark look. 'Listen. To. Me. The Glamour was dragged into oblivion by the Phaeron. People – friends – died in the process. For the sake of their memory, don't chase after everything that glitters or demands your attention.'

'But I thought the Glamour was gone for ever?' said Clara.

'Forever is a long time,' said the Doctor. 'But for things like the Glamour, it is seldom long enough.'

Acknowledgements

With thanks, as always, to Justin Richards, Steve Tribe, Lee Binding and Albert DePetrillo, and all the others involved in the publication of this book that I don't even know about.

And special mentions and love to Una McCormack and Gary Russell: accomplices, companions, comrades and friends in the telling of the Glamour Chronicles.

And finally Peter Capaldi and Jenna Coleman… for the wonderful Doctor and Clara.

BBC
DOCTOR WHO

Royal Blood
Una McCormack

ISBN 978-1-101-90583-8

The Grail is a story, a myth! It didn't exist on your world! It can't exist here!

The city-state of Varuz is failing. Duke Aurelian is the last of his line, his capital is crumbling, and the armies of his enemy, Duke Conrad, are poised beyond the mountains to invade. Aurelian is preparing to gamble everything on one last battle. So when a holy man, the Doctor, comes to Varuz from beyond the mountains, Aurelian asks for his blessing in the war.

But all is not what it seems in Varuz. The city-guard have lasers for swords, and the halls are lit by electric candlelight. Aurelian's beloved wife, Guena, and his most trusted knight, Bernhardt, seem to be plotting to overthrow their Duke, and Clara finds herself drawn into their intrigue…

Will the Doctor stop Aurelian from going to war? Will Clara's involvement in the plot against the Duke be discovered? Why is Conrad's ambassador so nervous? And who are the ancient and weary knights who arrive in Varuz claiming to be on a quest for the Holy Grail…?

An original novel featuring the Twelfth Doctor and Clara, as played by Peter Capaldi and Jenna Coleman

Also available from Broadway Books:

BBC

DOCTOR WHO

Big Bang Generation
Gary Russell

ISBN 978-1-101-90581-4

I'm an archaeologist, but probably not the one you were expecting.

Christmas 2015, Sydney, New South Wales, Australia

Imagine everyone's surprise when a time portal opens up in Sydney Cove. Imagine their shock as a massive pyramid now sits beside the Harbour Bridge, inconveniently blocking Port Jackson and glowing with energy. Imagine their fear as Cyrrus 'the mobster' Globb, Professor Horace Jaanson and an alien assassin called Kik arrive to claim the glowing pyramid. Finally imagine everyone's dismay when they are followed by a bunch of con artists out to spring their greatest grift yet.

This gang consists of Legs (the sexy come ... protection and firepower), Shortie (handl ... charge of excavation and history) and thei ... sure the universe isn't destroyed in an ex ... Bang look like a damp ...

And when someone accidentally reawak ... – which, Doc reckons, wasn't the wisest c ... things get a whole lot more c ...

An original novel featuring the Twelfth Docto ...